THIS DARK AND BLOODY GROUND

Tales of Frontier America

Book 1, *Maggie's Story*

Lori Roberts

Crecelius Haus Publishing, LLC

THIS DARK AND BLOODY GROUND

Tales of Frontier America

Book 1, Maggie's Story

Lori Roberts

Published in the United State of America
by
Crecelius Haus Publishing, LLC

ISBN:ebook: 978-1-7322492-6-4

ISBN: Soft cover: 978-1-7370597-0-7

First Printing September 2019

AUTHOR'S NOTE:
This is a work of fiction. Names characters, places and incidents are either
the product of the author's imagination or are used fictiously, and any resemblance to actual persons living or dead, business establishments, events, or
locales is entirely coincidental.

Dedication

To my 4th Great-grandfather, Otto Rudolph Crecelius, who immigrated from Reichelsheim, Germany to Philadeplphia, Pennsyvlvania in 1764. Soon after arriving in Philadelphia, his wife died during childbirth. In 1766, he married Marie Elizabeth Diederle Crecelius, my 4th Great-grandmother.

In 1782, they arrived in Washington County, North Carolina, which later became Tennessee. Their migration from Philadelphia, Maryland, the Shenandoah Valley of Virginia, and finally to the Wautaga area of the State of Franklin were the inspiration for this book.

Otto's youngest son, Jacob, was my 3rd Great-grandfathcr, who left Washington County, North Carolina, to arrive in Milltown, Indiana, where my Crecelius ancestors lived and where I grew up.

Jacob, and his wife, Christena, were the inspiration for Jacob and Christena Diele in this story.

Finally, to Gregkeln Diele, born 1452 in Germany, before the Diele name was Latinized to Krekel, then Crecelius. I'm the seventeenth generation from this ancestor.

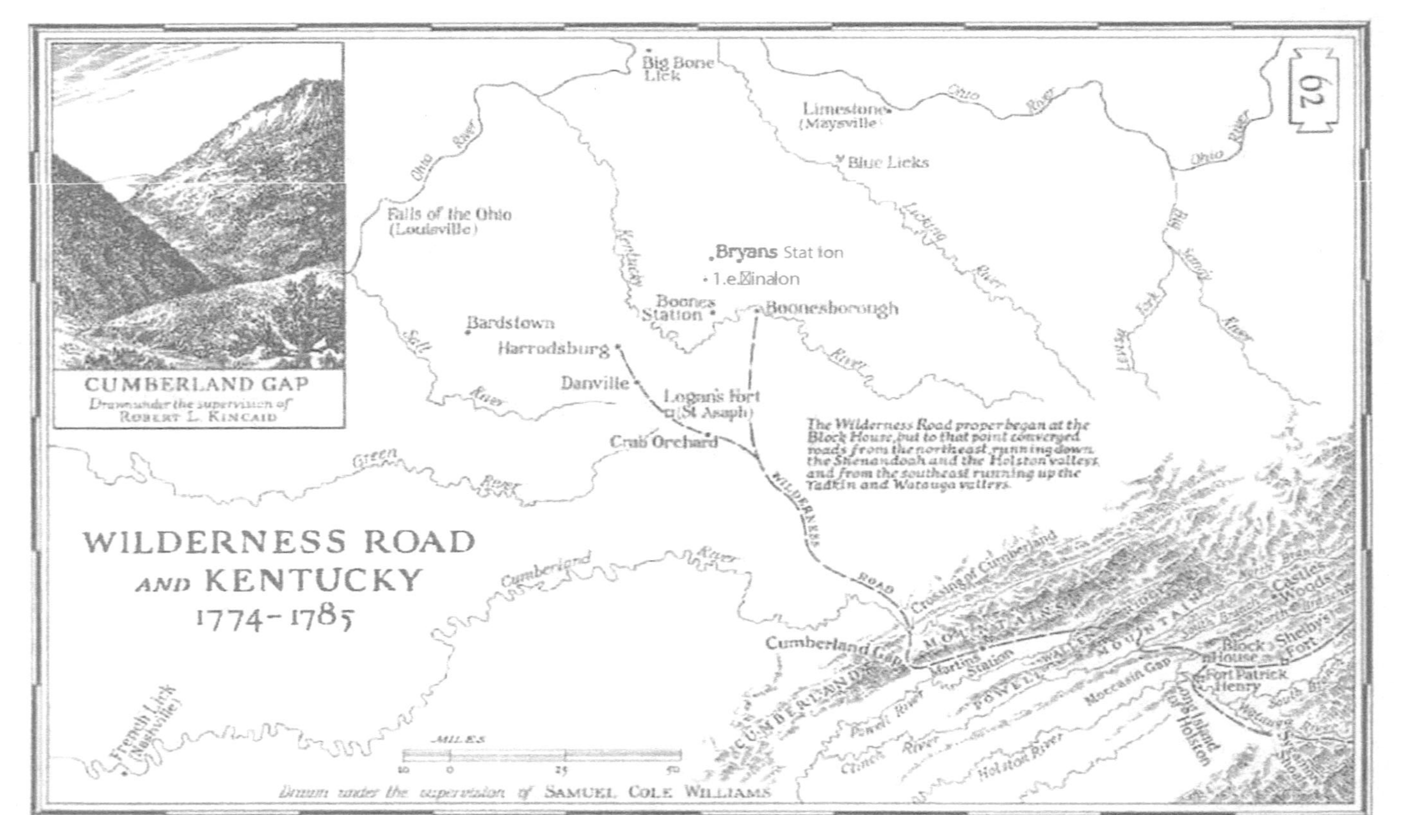
WILDERNESS ROAD
AND KENTUCKY
1774-1785
Drawn under the supervision of SAMUEL COLE WILLIAMS
CUMBERLAND GAP
Drawn under the supervision of ROBERT L. KINCAID
The Wilderness Road proper began at the Block House, but to that point converged roads from the northeast, running down the Shenandoah and the Holston valleys, and from the southeast running up the Yadkin and Watauga valleys.
Big Bone Lick
Limestone (Maysville)
Blue Licks
Falls of the Ohio (Louisville)
Bryans Station
Lexington
Boones Station
Boonesborough
Bardstown
Harrodsburg
Danville
Logan's Fort (St Asaph)
Crab Orchard
WILDERNESS ROAD
Crossing of Cumberland
Cumberland Gap
Martins Station
CUMBERLAND MOUNTAINS
POWELL MOUNTAIN
WALDEN MOUNTAIN
Moccasin Gap
Castle's Woods
Block House
Shelby's Fort
Fort Patrick Henry
Long Island of Holston
French Lick (Nashville)
Ohio River
Kentucky River
Licking River
Green River
Cumberland River
Salt River
Powell River
Clinch River
Holston River
Watauga River
MILES
10   0   25   50

Cast of Characters

Anna Magdelena"Maggie" Diele

Jacob and Christena Diele- Maggie's parents

Wilhelm Diele- Brother of Maggie.

Evan and Lydia McCampbell- Scottish immigrants

Mary Katherine McCampbell-daughter of Evan and Lydia

Thomas and Abigail Grundy

Anson and Josiah Grundy- sons of Thomas and Abigail

Lazarus and Polly- slaves of the Grundy family.

Daniel and Rebecca Boone

Cherokee Cast of Characters:

Hisgidihi (Five Killer)- son of Nanye'hi and Kingfisher

Nanye'hi ("One who goes about"), known in English as Nancy Ward (c. 1738 – 1822), was a Beloved Woman and political leader of the Cherokee.

Bryant Ward- Nancy Ward's Scots-Irish husband/trader

Usdi Alisoqualdi-Little Bear- Adopted mother of Maggie

Degataga- husband of Little Bear

Ahyoka- (meaning- She brought happiness) Maggie's Cherokee name

Oukonunaka- Cherokee warrior

Awiagina- Elder woman who Maggie calls "Grandmother"

Tayanita and Galilani- The friends of Maggie/Ahyoka

Mohe, Atohi, and Galegenoh- friends of Oukonunaka

Atsadi and Ayita- Uncle and Aunt of Oukonunaka

Chapter 1

Culpeper, Virginia
September 1775

Twelve-year old Anna Magdelena Diele, "Maggie" to her family, counted the different calls from the mockingbird that was perched in the sweetgum tree. The leather journal she'd written in earlier lay across her lap. The soft bedroll made of her quilt, tick mattress, and pillow were all that remained in her bedroom.

Below her window, her parents were deep in conversation. Her mind wandered from the mockingbird's change of calls while she eavesdropped on her parents' discussion. She knew better but couldn't help herself.

In the morning at first light, weeks of planning, packing, and praying would see progress. The sale of her family's home and belongings caused her mother much worry, since it was for a tract of unseen land in the wilderness. The opening of land in faraway Kentucke was the reason for the move by the Diele family. Jacob learned at the conference of Sycamore Shoals, the Transylvania Company from Virginia had purchased over two million acres of land from the Cherokee Indians. Families were eager to move into the new lands and purchase their 640-acre tracts from land speculators.

The move wasn't without danger, as word from the frontier told of Indian attacks within the land of Kentucke, now a county of the Commonwealth of Virginia.

Maggie's father, Jacob Diele, had sold two of their four horses for the two large beasts inside the stone barn.

The oxen would be able to pull the wagon over the mountains and through rough terrain.

"Will, Papa said you'll be leading the oxen. Mayhap you'll have a hand in naming them."

Wilhelm, two years younger than Maggie, hid his face behind his hat when Peter Mueller came to harness Samson and Delilah earlier in the day. She reminded him only babies cried at such things.

The thought of walking over miles of wilderness seemed exciting to Will. He'd yet to feel the leather of his brogans thinned from weeks of walking beside a wagon.

The unknown didn't frighten Maggie as it did her mother, Christena Diele. Twenty years earlier, as a young immigrant from Nauheim, Germany, she'd seen the unknown from the porthole of the ship, The Patience.

The moans of sick passengers rising from the hold of the ship were daunting as the churning sea tossed the ship for six harrowing weeks, all the while Christena's parents nursed her ill baby brother, Johannes. The toddler's lifeless form would join countless others who perished while crossing the Atlantic. Wrapped in his father's wool jacket, Johannes was lowered overboard to face a burial at sea. It was a sight Maggie's mother wouldn't forget.

Six months earlier, with trepidation, she'd relented to her husband, Jacob, when he spoke of purchasing a tract of land from the newly settled Boonesborough, in Kentucke.

Their two-story house, constructed of log and stone, was sold to Karl Eddleman, a middle-aged immigrant from Hamburg, Germany. His wife and two sons stood like stone columns, unable to converse in English.

Maggie hoped the Eddleman boys would appreciate her rope bed and tick mattress. Will's bed made a fine gift for their cousin, Anna Diederle. Maggie smiled thinking how her eyes lit up like two fireflies when her father delivered the bedstead to his brother-in-law's cabin.

Lost in thought, Maggie had forgotten where the mockingbird had gotten in its repertoire of calls. Just as well, as her mother called for her to fetch her brother from the barn. It was time to bid farewell to her aunts, uncles, and cousins who were waiting with tear-stained cheeks.

October 4th, 1775

Jacob Diele hitched the oxen to the wagon. He hoped the trade he'd made with Andrew O'Brien was a good one. He checked and double checked the yoke.

Maggie watched from her perch atop the wagon seat. Her small hands held her doll, Elizabetha Margaretha, tightly. The wooden doll mayhap could ride inside the wagon, for safe keeping. As of late, Maggie had less time for Elizabetha, her only doll. There was much work to do to ready for such an adventure as this.

The Diele family had been up before daylight to load the last of their possessions. A small spinning wheel, wooden crates filled with provisions, items needed for Christena's medicine chest, and their bedding were placed inside the tightly packed wagon.

In a pouch made for Christena to wear on her back, the pewter plates and cups, along with a teacup and saucer, were wrapped within scraps of cloth.

Jacob's axe, fro, seeds for planting in Kentucke, and carpenter tools needed to build a new homestead, were arranged to keep enough room for the family to take refuge under the wagon's cover.

They'd soon travel down the bumpy Great Wagon Road, crossing small streams and rough terrain. Other families in similar wagons would join the Diele's. Maggie felt a surge of excitement wondering what their daughters were like. It would be nice to have a new friend so far from home.

She looked at the homespun frock of linsey woolsey her mother fashioned for the trip over the mountains. It was a far cry from the finery she'd always seen her mother wear, save for the days she worked in her garden. Even in the plain dress and shawl, Christena Diele was a handsome woman. Maggie had overheard Peter Mueller tell his indentured servant just those words the afternoon they delivered the new wagon wheels.

Maggie hopped down from the seat, following her mother into the empty house. She watched in silence as her mother stood in front of the stone fireplace, her eyes pooling with tears. The gathering room was her mama's favorite room inside their two-story stone and log house. Many a time she'd entertained neighbors and family with their fine pewter tableware.

"Are you sad, Mama?" Maggie slipped her arm around her mother's tiny waist.

"Yes, poppet, I reckon so." Christena touched the hand-hewn mantle in admiration. Jacob spent many a long hour laboring over the piece. There wasn't a finer one in the whole town.

"No sense crying over such things. Your papa will fashion a nicer one once we've settled in Kentucke."

Maggie followed her mother out the front door. For the first time in her life, she watched her turn a long metal key in the padlock on the door.

Maggie clutched her wooden doll as she and Will took their place beside the wagon. She knew it was time to part with childish things, being on the cusp of young womanhood. It wouldn't hurt, she thought, for something to remind her of home. Around her neck, Maggie kept her journal fastened with a hemp rope and small lead pencil. She had two, both gifts from her aunt for the long trip. She kept her extra inside the wagon.

The cow, hitched to the back of the wagon with a tight rope sauntered along, bawling for its calf that Jacob had sold to their neighbor, Nicholaus Creech.

The bells hanging from the necks of the oxen clanked in a comforting cadence as they trudged along the dirt road from Culpeper southward toward Abingdon. Maggie and Will rode atop the spotted mare, Betsy, while Christena rode Jacob's horse, Saul. Once the family arrived at the Block House, they would sell the wagon and pack all their goods on the backs of the horses and oxen.

The Wagon Road, well-worn from years of wagons traveling north to deliver the mail, carried the Diele family away from the only home Maggie and Will had known.

October 10, 1775

The cold rain blew against the wagon canvas. The Diele family had traveled almost twelve miles before a sudden storm caused them to stop for the day. Christena and the children climbed into the wagon to stay out of the pouring rain. Lightning flashed across the sky. The wind howled and blew against the canvas as Jacob tied the animals to a nearby tree. In the distance, the booms of thunder echoed.

Jacob pushed aside the canvas flap, climbed inside, joining his wife and children. He reached into his vest and brought out the small pocket watch he kept on a leather braided fob. At four o'clock, the sky resembled the hours of dusk. Dark, foreboding clouds swirled overhead, and the sound of thunder surrounded the tiny wagon and its inhabitants. Water beat against the canvas top and rivulets ran down the sides.

"Papa, will the wind blow the wagon over?" Maggie's heart leaped in her chest as a strong wind gust rocked the wagon.

"No, poppet. The Almighty will calm the storm, don't fret." Jacob cupped Maggie's chin in his leathery hand.

Christena brought forth a muslin pouch containing the leftovers they would eat for the evening meal. In the semi-darkness they ate strips of dried venison and bread. As another gust of windy rain hit the wagon, Maggie and Will scooted closer to their mother.

Jacob pulled the leather ties tight to keep the rain from soaking their possessions. He reached below the makeshift table and opened the pine box holding the first book he'd ever read, the family Bible.

Next, he took a pine knot from the tinder box and drew out the fatwood. Jacob drew his whittling knife and shaved a sliver to put in a small pewter bowl. With two striking pieces made of iron, an ember caught fire within the pile of resinated wood shavings. The sooty smoke rose above their heads and a soft flickering glow illuminated the confines of the wagon.

The family sat on a soft pile of blankets for the Bible reading and evening prayers. This night, amid the rumbles of thunder, he opened the Bible and read from the book of Psalms.

Maggie's mind wandered as she listened to her father's soft voice read scripture in the glow of the lantern's light. She heard a hoot owl in the tree above them "hoo hooting" to anyone who'd listen.

When their father closed the large book, Maggie, Will, and their mother bowed their heads and held the hand of the person next to them.

Maggie tried to keep her eyes closed, but a rustling noise outside the wagon caught her attention. Her father didn't seem to notice because his prayer continued. The hoot owl went silent as Maggie strained to hear the evening sounds on the other side of the canvas.

A few moments later, Jacob said "amen", and his hand reached for Old Nell, the musket he carried for protection and killing game along the trail.

"Shh," he warned, putting his finger to his lips. He unlaced the top ties of the canvas flap, taking his musket with him as he crawled through the opening.

Maggie and Will sat wide-eyed, like stone pillars, neither making a sound. They didn't want to disobey their father. Christena's gaze darted from the opening in the canvas to her children. She fiddled with the edge of her shawl as she tried her best to appear calm.

Maggie's heart thumped in her chest like a scared rabbit. She'd heard her father whisper to her mother that he saw a she-bear wandering along the creek some miles back.

Jacob appeared through the opening. A sigh of relief escaped Christena's lips.

"It was only a raccoon and her babes. I 'spect she's looking for a dry place to bed for the night." He put Old Nell in the corner by the butter churn.

Will and Maggie unrolled their bed for the night. The soft tick mattress smelled of home. Maggie pulled her coverlet up to her chin. The rain caused a chill throughout her body. Will followed suit, snuggling under the homespun coverlet.

"Goodnight, Mama, goodnight, Papa." Maggie pulled Elizabetha Margaretha close to her side.

"Goodnight, poppet. Rest well." Christena leaned over her children, kissing each on the forehead." Goodnight Will."

"Good night, Mama." Will's eyes were closed before he finished speaking.

Chapter 2

Jacob knew the trek to Abingdon wasn't without danger. He wrestled with bringing his family into the dangerous wilderness. His family was two days from joining the other settlers at John Anderson's Blockhouse near the Clinch River in Carter's Valley. He thought about the land waiting to be planted with corn, and the fine cabin he'd build once they reached their tract of land, but the stories of Indian attacks at Boonesborough caused him to wrestle with his decision. Word of Daniel Boone's son, James, and others in the party who were sent back to North Carolina for supplies, were ambushed and killed in 1773. It was something he couldn't get off his mind. He heard talk of it when he spoke to the land agent with the Transylvania Land Company.

Too restless to sleep, Jacob took a pouch of tobacco from the box inside his saddlebag. He clinched the end of the pipe between his teeth and poked his head outside the canvas cover. The rain had stopped for the night. He crawled out of the opened flap to smoke his pipe and check on the cow tethered to the back of the wagon.

As he smoked, he listened to the sound of frogs down by the creek. He heard the hoot owl again. The light from the full moon cast shadows on the woods beyond the trail. He couldn't shake off the feeling of eyes upon him. He'd felt it when they filled their water satchels earlier in the evening. He finished the last of his pipe, tamping the embers onto the wet ground.

Jacob rubbed the back of his neck, feeling his skin prickle. He climbed inside the wagon, pulling the leather ties tightly together. Old Nell sat against the wagon frame, loaded and ready, if needed. At first light, the Diele's would begin their descent into Carter's Valley.

Will led the oxen down the curving wagon path. Their bells jingled, signaling to the black birds their entrance into the dark woods as he swatted a switch at their hooves. The trees displayed colors of scarlet red, blazing orange, and brilliant yellow, full of chattering squirrels and blackbirds.

Jacob had taken over the reins, careful not to catch the top of the canvas on a low branch. Christena and Maggie led the horses in single file to keep from losing their footing on the steep hill. Once they arrived at the blockhouse, the wagon would be taken apart, the wood used to fashion two ox carts for carrying only the necessities into their new homeland of Kentucke.

Maggie walked beside the wagon and pulled her shawl around her shoulders. The air was sharp against her legs and the thin shift and skirt she wore. She kept a keen eye toward the woods as she pulled on the hemp rope tied to the brindle heifer.

Around her neck, the cord holding her memory book swayed to and fro. She'd written about the prospect of making a new friend once they arrived at Mr. Anderson's blockhouse.

She feared she'd see a painted face peering from behind one of the chestnut trees along the trail. Catching her mother's eye, Maggie noticed she looked tired. She knew her mother was strong, mayhap, her thoughts of home and the family she'd left behind weighed on her mind.

Tendrils of Christena's dark hair had worked their way loose from the tight bun under her mobcap. She kept pace with the wagon and tucked her hair back into her cap. She winked at Maggie and hummed a melody as she walked beside the oxen.

Culpeper was a fine town but talk of war with England worried Christena. She knew Jacob would answer the call to fight since he belonged to the militia. But his wanting to own land in the frontier caught hold of the wanderlust streak she thought he'd outgrown. Now, she would have to start all over again, with only the barest of necessities. No more frippery and finery, as she was accustomed.

Jacob allowed only what could be carried by pack animal or small cart for the trip. The wagon was small in comparison to others they had seen on the Wagon Road. Will and Maggie could bring one special item. Maggie chose her doll, and her journal, the latter didn't take up space since it hung around her neck. Maggie and Will had been taught to read and write by their mother. Many of the settlers traveling to Kentucke could only make their mark, a large X. Only a few more could read.

The Diele family had left their home with a small sum of British pounds and pieces of eight. They would need money to buy supplies. Jacob had made a living in Culpeper as a furniture maker and farmer. Some of his pieces were sold to the city's wealthier residents. Christena knew he would build her another fine home, once they were settled.

Will carried a slingshot whittled for him by his father on his last birthday. Like the Biblical shepherd boy, David, he carried a small pouch of smooth round stones in his pocket, in case his aim was needed. He had only shot a gun once, and it took him to the ground. Jacob promised he would have his own gun once he grew into it. He had a steady aim with his slingshot and could bring down small animals for their pelts and for the meat.

Jacob signaled time to stop for the evening. After they helped tie the animals to the wagon, Maggie and Will raced to the rushing stream nearby to fill buckets for their mother.

Christena mixed a cup of cornmeal and a cup of flour in a wooden bowl. She added salt and a teaspoon of soda. Using the last of the water in the canteen, she stirred the johnny cake batter.

Jacob built a fine cook fire and fetched the cast iron skillet from the wagon. Christena spooned a healthy portion of lard from the grease crock. She heard the giggles coming from the creek bank in the distance.

Down in the creek, Maggie waded up to her knees, enjoying the feel of the water rushing across her legs. Will reached for a slippery fish, losing his balance. He fell onto his backside, causing a large splash. Maggie bent into the creek and splashed her soaked brother. He reached out and pulled Maggie into the water. The pair splashed and dunked one another, unaware of a pair of dark eyes watching from across the bank.

"Maggie, Will, hurry with the water," Jacob called.

"Coming, Papa!" They grabbed their buckets and hurried back to the wagon.

In another day, they would reach the divide in the road where one way led south to the Yadkin Valley and the other to Abingdon and the Anderson Blockhouse. It was there they and the others would wait for Daniel Boone and his family to lead them through the Cumberland Gap.

Chapter 3

October 31st, 1775
Anderson Blockhouse, in southwestern Virginia.

The blockhouse sat on a rise above the road. Built in 1775 in Virginia's East Carter's Valley, it was the last haven for those migrating toward Kentucke. Designed to protect settlers from raids, it became a stopping place for pioneers migrating toward the Cumberland Gap.

Carter's Valley was situated between the North and South forks of the Holston River. The Indians were prone to attack the Holston settlements from the west and would most likely emerge from the Big Moccasin Gap and come straight up the valley. The settlers needed to keep the access to the valley open to prevent attacks on the Holston settlements.

A sight to behold, Maggie thought the blockhouse resembled two log cabins, one atop the other, and the top cabin over reached the lower. A large solid wood door with a rope attached to a small block of wood that could be pulled through the hole at night, kept the door locked from outsiders. She saw one small window in the whole structure, and presently, it was covered with an animal hide.

She remembered how the light streamed through the glass in the windows at their home in Culpeper. There was no reason to have a lock on the door, but things were different here.

All around the building were openings in the logs.

"Papa, why does the Blockhouse have all the holes in the walls?" Maggie asked.

Jacob turned to speak to the children, riding inside the swaying wagon. "The holes are cut so the long rifles and muskets can shoot through in case of attack."

"I bet Old Nell could kill all the savages." Will's enthusiasm drew reproach from his mother.

"Wilhelm, we should pray for their souls. I will hear no more of that talk." Christena's voice remained soft, but firm.

Maggie moved her brother out of the way, taking her place in the opening. She surveyed the blockhouse as the wagon turned up the rutted wagon trail.

Jacob explained the upper level had an equal number of rifle ports for the men to shoot down on any invaders. The openings would be closed with a block of wood when a gun port wasn't needed.

A large stone and mud fireplace, situated on the inside of the blockhouse, prevented the Indians from climbing up the chimney from outside and accessing the roof. The massive logs used to build the blockhouse fit together tightly by tongue and groove. No daub was used, and the house was tight and dry.

"Papa, why is the roof so steep?" Maggie wondered.

"Poppet, no Indian could stand atop the roof or shoot an arrow into it that would stay fixed on the spot. It is a matter of defense." Jacob switched the backside of the oxen as they pulled the family closer to the fortification.

A single plume of smoke danced from the chimney. On the outside, benches made from small logs lined the walls and a few men in fringed shirts and long breeches with tall knee boots stood as their wagon approached the blockhouse.

John Anderson, a large man, rising to a height of six foot-two inches and weighing upwards of two hundred pounds, wore a dark green frock coat and wool knee breeches. Tall leather boots covered his legs. His red hair and ruddy complexion resembled other Irish immigrants that lived in and around her home. He chatted with man who wore an animal skin hat.

Jacob halted the animals and the children jumped down from the back of the wagon. He helped Christena from her place on the seat. Together, she and the children walked beside the wagon as Jacob led the oxen to a hitching post. Will pulled his cap up to see the men coming to welcome the new arrivals.

A man dressed like an Indian came from behind the blockhouse. He carried a large musket in one hand and the carcass of a small doe across his shoulders. Will's wide eyes followed the man as he hung the deer from a rope strung over a tree. It was then they could see the insides of the deer had been removed, no doubt in the woods where the man brought the deer to the ground. He drew from his waist a long knife and proceeded with the process of removing the hide as blood dripped from the inside of the carcass.

Jacob led the family to a group of settlers gathered near a large cabin. A tall man in a tricorn hat made his way over to Jacob and welcomed him to the Anderson blockhouse.

Rebecca, bride of Colonel John Anderson, arrived in the spring of 1775 when he built the large blockhouse. She no doubt longed for female companionship, even if it be for a short time. She had a warm smile and pretty face. Christena noticed she appeared younger than Colonel Anderson.

"Welcome. Where have you traveled from?" John Anderson boomed.

Jacob extended his hand to the much taller Anderson and pumped it. "Jacob Diele's my name. This is my wife, Christena, and my young 'ins, Maggie and Will." He looked approvingly at his family. "We come from Culpeper."

"What news is there from the militia?" Anderson asked.

"Word from Boston last month was General Washington was holding siege over the British. Many of the good people of Culpeper are having to watch for Tory spies." He shook his head. "They be hard times."

"Yes, we have our fight with the savages and the bloody British." He spat a stream of tobacco and wiped his chin with his sleeve.

Maggie turned away from the spectacle. Tobacco chewing was detestable, but it was something she'd grow accustomed to from the looks of the men at the blockhouse.

Colonel Anderson led Jacob past the blockhouse and down to an area where a small barn connected to a corral where several horses and a few milk cows were chewing on grass.

"You can bring your stock here after you unhitch them. We take turns guarding and keeping a sharp eye out for Shawnee, Delaware, and Cherokee. We've been attacked as recent as last month. Shot a couple of Shawnees trying to steal our horses." Anderson wiped the sweat from his forehead with his sleeve. "Had to bury two good men on account of them. You keep your eye on your wife and young ones at all times."

"I have two muskets and my wife, Christena, is a true shot. My boy, Will, isn't as steady with the gun, but his aim with the slingshot could bring down a small doe or man, if need be."

"The savages should be making their move out of the valley to their winter camps. It's a mite colder but traveling through the mountains during the winter is safer for you."

Jacob prayed to God he was right. He walked back to the wagon where he'd left his wife and children. Rebecca Anderson had led Christena and Maggie to a lean-to that would be their home until Captain Boone returned from fetching his family and others from the Yadkin Valley in North Carolina. Will remained with the animals and the wagon.

Jacob called for Will to fetch the cow from the wagon as he unhitched the oxen and walked them to the corral. Will hurried to do as his father asked and led the cow down the path.

Christena surveyed the lean-to. She rested her hands on her hips, looking at the limbs and pine boughs used for a roof. She smiled at Rebecca. "It is fine. Thank you."

She pulled Maggie to her side, wondering what hardships still awaited them.

"The blockhouse is small, but if there is any danger about, you are to hurry to the door and have your husband bring his gun and ammunition with haste." Rebecca pulled the wool blanket around her shoulders as she walked with Christena to her wagon.

"My Jacob will set about tearing the wagon apart after it is unloaded. He plans to fashion us two ox carts to carry my spinning wheel and provisions."

"It's a far cry from what you left behind, but we make the best of our surroundings," Rebecca offered. She watched Christena and Maggie carry their items from the back of the wagon. "When you're finished getting settled, you can bring me any letters you want to post before you set off for Martin's Station. There isn't anyone taking the post to the settlers after you leave here."

"Oh, yes, thank you. I saved several sheets of writing tablet before we left Culpeper. I used it to wrap my tea cup and saucer." Christena took on a look of sorrow as she thought of the other dishes and cups she gave to her family before leaving their stone and log home.

"My husband will be going back to purchase supplies and send the posts back east. Good day, Mrs. Diele." She lifted the rope and block latch and went inside the warm blockhouse.

The Diele family settled into their temporary quarters. The items were removed from the wagon and placed inside the lean-to. Jacob set to work disassembling the wagon piece by piece. As soon as the shelter was finished, he would start building two ox carts for their larger possessions. The horses would be used to carry the rest of their belongings.

Jacob used canvas from the wagon to make two drapes. He carried limbs and covered them with the canvas to shield the family from the elements. At present, a good campfire and warm blankets kept the chill at bay. The daytime temperatures were tolerable, a blessing for the families living in lean-to shelters around the blockhouse. The large outdoor oven was a place where the women made their bread and other baked goods. The small cook fire used by day, was used at night to warm the Diele family and discourage wolves from wandering too close.

Maggie helped her mother put the johnnycake on the skillet. Mrs. Anderson had brought Christena a small crock of pumpkin butter, a treat, to spread on the cornmeal johnny cakes. Christena had enough flour to have bread sparingly. Cornmeal was more plentiful, and it fried up quicker on the iron skillet. The grease from the hog Jacob butchered in the spring was half gone from the pottery jar Christena used back home in Culpeper. The last of the dried venison was eaten at the evening meal.

Jacob promised a rabbit for dinner tomorrow. Maggie finished her supper and helped Christena wash off the pewter plates they'd brought from home.

After supper, the families gathered near the blockhouse to listen to fiddle music. The men who were assigned guard duty kept a sharp eye out for wild animals and Indians.

The Diele's had traveled for two weeks alone from their home in upper Virginia to the Holston Valley. Maggie and Will hadn't worried about Indian attacks on the Great Wagon Road, however, they had trouble closing their eyes on this first night at the blockhouse.

The sounds of animals in the surrounding woods and the fear of Indians made a restful slumber impossible. Jacob kept Old Nell close by while watching the lazy fire send a steady smoke trail into the sky. Similar scenes were visible at the other shelters around the encampment.

Jacob moved under the canvas roof, settling under the patchwork quilt covering his wife. He glanced over at a sleeping Maggie and Will and thanked the Lord above for protecting his family thus far. He hoped to reach Martin's Station before the snow fell in the mountains.

Chapter 4

"Halloo!" A voice shouted over the jangling bells attached to the horses' harnesses. A short-legged man with tan knee britches jumped down from the wagon seat. His red hair poked out from the sides of his wool cap like hay straws.

Maggie eyed the wagon as it slowed to a stop. Her father walked to the short-legged man and offered his hand.

"Jacob Diele's my name. This is my family." He pumped the man's stubby hand, and pointed over his shoulder to Christena, who pulled Maggie next to her. "Christena, my wife." She nodded politely. "My children, Maggie and Will."

Will tried to make himself taller by standing with his shoulders pulled back.

"The name's Evan McCampbell. My missus, Lydia, is feelin' a mite poorly. She's layin' in the wagon." He waved his thumb toward the wagon. "She'll be feelin' fine as frog's hair by the morrow." His Scottish brogue boomed from his short frame.

"I'm sorry to hear that. Any young'ins?" Jacob saw a pair of small boots walk from behind the wagon as soon as he asked.

"This be my daughter, Mary Katherine." The girl appeared the same age as Maggie. The girls traded a quick wave between them.

"Mr. McCampbell, mayhap I could look in on your wife?" Christena stepped from behind her husband. She let go of the protective grip she had on Maggie.

"Don't see what it'd hurt none. Thank ye, ma'am." He took his cap off his head, tucking it under his arm as Christena walked passed him.

Maggie followed her mother to the back of the Mc-Campbell's wagon. She pulled the strings of her mob cap around her head.

Christena found the canvas opened, exposing the inside. Lydia McCampbell lay on a makeshift pallet beneath a patchwork quilt. Her eyes were closed, but she opened them slowly when Christena spoke.

"Mrs. McCampbell, I'm Christena Diele. My husband and I are part of the group heading into Kentucke. Is there anything I can do to help you?"

Lydia pulled herself up with all her strength. "I must look a fright. I'm a mite weak, but it's expected. I'm with child."

Maggie watched her mother and Mrs. McCampbell exchange a telling glance. She wondered why grown folks always reverted to this quiet communication.

"I'm sure you'll be fit as a fiddle by the morrow. I have some ginger root in my wagon, should you be wanting a cup of ginger tea. Good day, Mrs. McCampbell."

"Aye, thank you, Mrs. Diele. I'll be paying 'yer family a proper visit soon."

Maggie followed behind her mother.

"Mama, will Mrs. McCampbell's baby be alright?"

Maggie remembered the small baby her parents had buried last winter. Christian Heinrich was a wee babe of four days old, his body too weak after the ordeal of childbirth. Her mother had been melancholy for most of the spring and summer. Her question caused a forlorn expression to appear over her mother's usual pleasantness.

"I'm sure Mrs. McCampbell is just tired from the journey, poppet." She cupped her hand under Maggie's chin, her touch gentle and loving.

Maggie stood by the wagon as her father and Evan Mc-Campbell greeted the driver of the second wagon. It looked as if the group waiting on Captain Boone grew by two more families.

Will hurried to catch up to his father. He hoped there were boys in the new arrivals.

"Good day to you." The driver jumped from his seat, extending his hand to both Jacob and Evan. His sandy blonde hair was pulled into a ponytail and tied with a small black ribbon. He wore a tri-cornered hat with a yellow band along the edge. His attire reminded Maggie of a militia member back home in Culpeper.

"I'm Thomas Grundy. Pleased to make your acquaintance." His grip was strong as he shook the hands of Mr. McCampbell and Jacob. Tipping his hat to Christena, he continued his introductions. "This is my wife, Abigail."

Christena joined her husband in making formal introductions. The proprietor of the blockhouse had left earlier to check his traps in the woods with another man. Rebecca Anderson pulled her shawl around her and stepped outside to welcome the new arrivals to her home.

The Grundy wagon party consisted of Thomas, Abigail, and young sons, Anson and Josiah. A young servant stood near her mistress. The girl appeared to be older than Maggie by a year or two. Another servant, an older male, stood with a milk cow tied to a short hemp rope.

Maggie had seen slaves in her town with their masters before leaving, and now meeting a couple, she wondered what it was like to have someone do your chores.

"Come along, Maggie." Christena adjusted the straw hat perched atop her head. The small day cap she wore underneath covered her dark black hair.

"Mama, when will we be joining Captain Boone?" Maggie helped her mother get the leftover johnny cakes from breakfast out of the wooden box in which she kept the food store.

"Mr. Anderson expects him today or tomorrow." She spread a patchwork coverlet of muslin on the ground for Maggie and Will.

Lunch was soon prepared—apples from their tree back home, strips of dried beef jerky, and left-over johnny cakes from breakfast. Christena filled two pewter mugs with cider from an earthen jug and handed them to her children.

The new settlers were busy making shelters for their families. The McCampbell's and Grundy's would tear their wagons down to make carts like Jacob's. What parts could be sold would fund items needed to take into Kentucke.

Mr. Anderson had few supplies at the blockhouse but was expecting a wagon of goods coming with Boone and the settlers from the Yadkin Valley. Supplies were running low, and the much-needed supplies would carry them through most of the winter.

Maggie and Will walked over to where the children of the McCampbell's and Grundy's sat on tree stumps being used as chairs. The Grundy boys were about Will's age, and both had slingshots like his. At the sight, Will's eyes danced with the prospect of having boys to do things with instead of his older, bossy sister.

Maggie smiled at Mary Katherine McCampbell who looked like a scared doe. Her mother was trying to help her father drag limbs to make a temporary shelter. Her rounded belly protruded from beneath her shift and skirt. Maggie came over to Mary Katherine and sat down on the log beside her.

"Hello, I'm Maggie. When is your mama going to birth her babe?"

Mary Katherine looked over to where her parents were busy working on the lean-to. "I don't know for sure. Mother says it will come in Kentucke. She feels poorly most of the time."

"Do you hope the babe will be a sister? I've always wanted a sister." Maggie looked over at Will.

"I don't rightly know, t'will be a blessing either way, mother says." Her voice carried the same Scottish brogue as her father, something Maggie thought was pretty to the ears.

Mary Katherine was more womanly looking to Maggie than she. She was wearing stays, but her development was obvious. Maggie had only recently taken to wearing her first stays. The tightness was unpleasant, but she could no longer wear just a thin cotton shift without a modesty kerchief. She also admired Mary Katherine's deep green eyes and flaxen hair.

Maggie hadn't seen herself in a looking glass for a few weeks, but she knew she wasn't pretty like Mary Katherine. She had dark hair, like her mama, and dark brown eyes like her papa.

"Would you like to see my doll? I brought her all the way from Culpeper."

Mary Katherine smiled. "You have a doll with you? I had a doll once, but our house burned to the ground. My doll, Lollie, burned up." She looked sad again.

"Oh, I'm sorry. Elizabetha is inside our lean-to." She hurried across the way to where her mother was writing a letter to her aunt.

She returned carrying the wooden peg doll. Maggie was proud of the dress and underthings her mother had made for Elizabetha this last Christmas.

Mary Katherine held out her hands to take the doll. She turned the doll to admire the workmanship of her clothing.

"She is so pretty. I wish I had something to remind me of home. Mother says I'm too old for such things."

Maggie felt a twinge of embarrassment at the comment. She knew she was getting to be a young woman, and she should put such things away. She accepted the doll back from Mary Katherine.

"Yes, I suppose. I felt she was my only friend, until you." Maggie clasped her new friend's hand. She was glad for the McCampbell's joining their group.

Jacob took his turn at guard watch, listening for different sounds coming from the dark woods around the fortification, as well as watching the stock inside the corral. A sudden movement near the corral caught his attention, and upon closer inspection, he saw two young Indian boys sneaking toward the corral. Tomahawks hung from the waist of their breechcloths. Jacob pulled his gun up to his shoulder. Old Nell was primed and ready to fire.

A shot rang out nearby, causing the two Indian boys to drop once again to the ground. Jacob watched as they darted as fast as their legs would carry them toward the woods.

Jacob put his musket beside him, seeing Evan McCampbell shoulder his musket, coming from behind the back of the blacksmith's barn.

"They be sneakin' into the corral—filthy savages—they are." He pulled a small silver flask from his vest pocket. The contents dribbled down his red whiskers.

"I 'spect we've not seen the last of them." Jacob listened to the squirrels barking in the trees nearby.

"Something's moving through the woods. We best alert Captain Anderson of the two young Indians." Jacob had an uneasy feeling about them.

"I'll be talkin' to Captain Anderson straight away, you be keeping your attention on the animals." Evan took another swig from his flask before leaving his post.

Maggie sat cross-legged on the makeshift bedroll over a bed of straw. She took out her journal and began writing about life inside the blockhouse. The small beeswax candle gave off marginal light and her eyes strained to see the words she penned in the journal.

November 3, 1775

Today I helped Mama mend Papa's shirt. She says I have a neat stitch. Will and the Grundy boys wandered into the woods alone with their slingshots. They returned with a rabbit and tongue lashing from Papa and Mr. Grundy. Will helped Papa finish building the two ox carts. The wheels are a bit off, Papa says. Mrs. Grundy and her servant, Polly, visited with us today. She is a fine lady. I asked the servant if she would like to see Elizabetha. I don't expect servants have such things. She turned her upside down to see the underthings. She acted scared when I spoke to her. She said she didn't have a doll. I asked her where her mama was, but she couldn't tell me. Mr. Grundy bought her at an auction near Williamsburg. I would be terribly sad if someone took me from my mama and papa.

Christena asked Maggie to put out the flame and get to sleep. She put her journal under her blanket and fell asleep. While she and her brother slept under the canopy of pine boughs and chestnut limbs, Jacob Diele kept watch over his family until he, too, fell asleep.

Chapter 5

Thomas Grundy, Evan McCampbell, and Jacob Diele stood at the bank of the Clinch River. Its current moved steady and proved it could be easily crossed. Their attention was diverted to the sound of leaves rustling from the hill above them. Each man carried a musket and powder for protection since the incident with the young Indians at the corral.

The sight of Will and the Grundy boys rushing down to the river's edge brought a twinge of fear to Jacob.

"What's the matter, Will?" he asked.

"Captain Boone arrived just now, Pa. He brought more people with him," Will said, catching his breath.

Evan McCampbell let out a holler. "Well praise be! It's not a wee bit too soon. Let's be getting back up to meet Captain Boone."

The men hurried up the bank and followed the boys back to the blockhouse.

The families from North Carolina looked weary from their journey through the mountains to reach Carter's Valley.

Daniel Boone was a tall man. He was outfitted in buckskin breeches and a fringed hunting shirt. His auburn hair was tied at the nape of his neck with a leather cord. He stood taller than Jacob, but not as tall as Mr. Grundy. His piercing blue eyes held the wonders of the lands he'd mapped and explored the past two years.

He shook Mr. Anderson's hand and pounded him on the back. The men of the settlement were glad to see the pack animals and small wagons filled with much needed supplies—including barrels of flour, molasses, and cornmeal. Dried beef and salt, gathered at the licks nearby, were wrapped in brown paper and tied with hemp rope.

Captain Boone brought with him his wife, Rebecca, a pretty woman with dark hair and eyes like Christena's, but a few years older. Along with the Boone's were their children and several Boone and Bryan family members from the Yadkin Valley. This would be his last trip through the Gap until spring.

November 5th, 1775

The day before leaving Anderson's blockhouse, the men spent their time making bullets. Jacob and Christena put the round balls and black gun powder into paper cartridges then Jacob placed them into a leather satchel next to the powder horn that hung from a leather strap across his chest.

Will practiced his aim behind the corral with the Grundy boys. The three had been taking target practice at a fat pumpkin propped atop the fence post.

Maggie and Mary Katherine spent the final day at the blockhouse helping their mothers prepare the bread and johnny cakes to be eaten on the trail. A good amount of dried venison remained in Christena's provisions. There were still walnuts and chestnuts in sacks that could be roasted over the fire. Food would be rationed, and portions cut down while traveling.

The Anderson blockhouse was a flurry of activity as the pioneers packed the last of their provisions on the backs of the oxen and mules.

The ox carts were loaded, and animals were tied together using long hemp ropes. The children would be given the task of leading the animals along the trail. Maggie and Will were given cattail wadding to line the bottoms of their shoes since most of the leather soles were worn to bare.

Everyone was readying to leave, each with their own tasks. The weather had turned that morning, making the families even more eager to leave. Jacob pulled the collar of his jacket up around his neck. He folded the two parts of canvas from the lean-to and put them in the bottom of each ox cart.

Mrs. Anderson promised to mail the two letters Christena Diele left for her parents and sister.

"God be with you, Mrs. Diele, and watch over you on the trail." Mrs. Anderson hugged Christena tight.

"Thank you for your kindness, Mrs. Anderson. I hope someday to see you again."

Maggie tied her journal around her neck and waited for the adults to finish their goodbyes. She looked to the front of the line of horses, mules, and oxen loaded full of the settlers' life possessions. She carried a small leather pouch on her back with Elizabetha and her extra clothing. She pulled her wool blanket around her shoulders to keep the chill from snaking around her body. She was thankful for the new woolen socks her mother had fashioned for her before their journey.

Will stood beside his father, eager to lead the brindle heifer. He and Josiah Grundy secured their slingshots on their hips by a hemp rope. Both were ready to answer the call to duty, if needed.

Finally, Captain Boone put his musket over his shoulder and began the longest part of the journey into Kentucke and the Wilderness Trail. They followed Daniel Boone and family to the last fortification before crossing over Moccasin Gap and along the Great Warriors Path before crossing over the Cumberland Gap into Kentucke.

Chapter 6

November 8, 1775

The pioneers traveled for two days before reaching Martin's Station. The cool autumn air was a blessing to the animals carrying packages and those making their way over the mountains.

Maggie rode atop one of the Diele's horses. On its back were seeds of corn and oats packed within the saddlebags for planting once the Diele family reached their land claim near Boonesborough.

Will led one of the oxen pulled carts loaded with clothing and food stores. The other ox cart contained the iron skillets, pots, pewter plates and mugs made of stoneware. Christena's prized spinning wheel, wrapped into two parts with the scraps of canvas drape, lay atop the mound of goods. Each traveler trudged through the thick underbrush and cool dirt on the trace. Buffalo and deer had traveled the same well-worn path for centuries, and now the Cherokee, Delaware, and Shawnee traveled from the Warrior's Path to the south using many of the same trails as the pioneers.

Dark clouds gathered, and the tall trees of the woods formed a natural canopy, blocking out what sun's rays shone on this gray day.

The travelers kept their chatter mainly to the person walking beside them. As they walked through the dense forest, eyes were always watching for quick movement or a call of a bird in the distance.

Daniel Boone signaled a halt in the progression. The happy chatter ended abruptly.

"What be the matter?" Evan McCampbell said in almost a whisper, rubbing the brassy stubble on his cheek. He pulled his musket from the sling across his back.

"Something in the distance must've caught Captain Boone's eye." Jacob held his musket close, a cartridge already loaded.

Maggie slid off her horse and searched her father's dark eyes. "Papa are there savages ahead?" She slid her hand in his.

"I don't know, daughter. Go back to your horse and put your brother on Betsy's back."

Maggie did as she was told. Will climbed on the horse behind her, putting his arms around Maggie's waist. She could feel him trembling, or maybe it was her own knees shaking. She searched the faces of those around her. A mourning dove called to its mate in the hickory tree nearby. Not a word was spoken as they waited for word from Daniel Boone.

The band of travelers didn't have long to wait. Daniel rode his chestnut colored mare back through the line. Every few families, he warned the men to have their muskets at the ready as Martin's Station would be the next stop. The area was known for Indian attacks on settlers traveling through the Powell Mountains.

Martin's Station, Virginia

The pioneers reached the station before sundown on November 6th. The fortification was much larger than Anderson's blockhouse. The tall palisade fence enclosed the cabins, ordinary—also known as tavern—and cabins for officers. A blacksmith, gunsmith, and corrals were on the outside of the enclosure. Camp would be made for the night.

The boys led the stock to the creek while campfires were started by the women. Maggie and Mary Katherine, along with the Boone daughters, carried water back for their water jugs to be filled.

Maggie was about the same age as Jemima Boone, the pretty light auburn-haired beauty. She seemed to have her hands full helping her mother with her younger brothers and sisters. She was told the oldest sister, Susannah, was married and already living at Boonesborough with her husband, William.

Rebecca Boone shared a bit of bear bacon with Christena. She took the slab of meat and cut off several slices. She placed the slices in the skillet over the crackling fire. The dark, greasy slices sizzled next to the cornmeal cakes. The smell soon drifted throughout the camp.

Maggie sat on a tree stump, watching similar scenes from the surrounding camp sites.

While everyone went about normal activities, the ever-present awareness of savages attacking the camp kept everyone anxious and on guard.

Christena packed away the last of the cooking wares as Jacob took the family Bible from the box. Maggie and Will pulled their blankets around their shoulders as they listened to their father read about Moses leading the Israelites from the wilderness. Maggie wondered if the Egyptians looked like the Indians who pursued the white settlers trying to get to Kentucke.

Maggie listened to Mr. Grundy play his fiddle from his campsite. Other fiddles joined in, their soft lullaby ushered Maggie and Will into a deep slumber.

Chapter 7

The trek from Martin's Station through the Cumberland Gap was indeed the most dangerous of the entire journey. The terrain became more treacherous as the group descended from the mountains. Everyone walked down the trace, choosing their steps and steadying the pack animals.

The temperature dropped during the day. The brown leaves rustled in the crisp autumn air as crows cackled in the chestnut and elm trees.

Maggie led Betsy while listening to a lonely whippoorwill calling for its mate.

With no sign of Indians, the settlers became less anxious as they traveled toward Kentucke. They climbed up hills that were almost the height of the Clinch Mountains and wound their way around and down a terrain tumbled with rocks.

Descending into Powell's Valley, the settlers crossed Dick's River. The icy water was a shock to Maggie as she led Betsy across the creek. Will led Otto, the Ox that pulled the first cart. Behind him was Peter, the other Diele's ox. Peter followed Otto into the creek.

The current was swift below Maggie's feet. Waves of water splashed against her thighs as she stepped down into a shallow. She looked behind her as Will bent down to collect a few of the smooth stones he spied for his slingshot. The hoof of the ox he led came down on his foot, wedging it between two larger rocks. He cried out as he went into the water, unable to stand. The ox moved along, pulling the heavy cart over Will.

The long line of pack horses and animals came to a halt as Jacob and Christena hurried to free their son before he was covered by the flow of the Dick's River. Evan Mc-Campbell called to his daughter, Mary Katherine, to hold tight to the horses as he forced his short legs through the water to where the Diele's were working to loosen Will's foot.

Maggie stood in the middle of the river, the water slapping against her back. She held tight to the rope on her horse. The rest of the animals, tied together, tried to cross the river without their owner.

When Mr. McCampbell reached Will, he grabbed the boy from under his arms and pulled him up as his parents hurried to free his foot. After much worry, the boy was freed from the clutches of the large stones of the Dick's River. His mother pulled him to her breast, hugging and kissing his face. The cold water soaked Will to the skin. Maggie finally took in a gulp of air, having held her breath unknowingly as her parents worked to free their son.

"God bless you, Evan." Jacob embraced the stocky Scotsman, pounding his back twice.

"Ye be doin' the same for me, I 'spect. 'Twas nothing." He shook off his hat and put it back on his unruly red hair.

As soon as the Diele's crossed Dick's River, Christena fetched one of the blankets from the ox cart for Will to wrap around his shoulders. He shivered, trying to keep his teeth from chattering.

As sudden as the incident happened, it was over, and everyone continued across the river through a large cane brake. The stalks were taller than any man on the trail.

It was here they met two hunters returning from the salt licks beyond Twitty's Fort. Salt was a needed commodity and necessity for the preservation of meat. The animals had long made their migrations to the salt licks, another reason for the buffalo and deer paths throughout the mountains.

Daniel Boone spoke to the hunters, having known them from earlier days. Ezra Yeager and James Gassaway were dressed from head to foot in buckskin. Both men looked like they had been bedding with wild hogs and smelled worse.

Captain Boone learned they had been on the trail of three Shawnee warriors who had stolen their horses. They had waited until the three had stopped to make camp, and when they finally fell asleep, Yeager and Gassaway shot and killed them and lifted their scalps.

They told of Shawnee and Cherokee raids near Boonesborough, but the people there were safe. Rebecca Boone and the Boone contingent were relieved to hear it.

Maggie noticed one of the hunters had a collection of locks of black hair hanging from his waist. As she looked closer, it caused her to recoil in horror. She tugged her mother's linen shirt. "Mama, they have —"

"Yes," Christena said, unable to take her eyes off the spectacle. "Our people are no better than the savage." She pulled Maggie closer, touching her long tresses.

The first snowfall arrived the twenty-fifth of November. The pioneers donned their woolen blankets, shawls, and quilts. Maggie and her mother rode along on Betsy and Saul, while Jacob and Will led the oxen through the massive cane brake ahead. In some places, Maggie couldn't see what lie beyond to her left or right.

The party of settlers would soon divide to go their separate ways--Harrodsburg to the west, and the rest of the party to the north to Boonesborough. The distance between Harrodsburg and Boonesborough was near 30 miles. It might as well be 300 miles for the wives who would be confined to the fort, hurrying to throw up a shelter while the husbands took to the woods to fell the large trees needed to build cabins.

The snow mixed with ice pellets stung Maggie's face as she led Betsy. Her toes were stinging from the cold and damp seeping through the soles of her shoes despite the cattail wadding.

Lydia McCampbell had regained her strength and rode beside Christena along the bank of Otter Creek. The two women had become good friends since their meeting at the blockhouse. Maggie couldn't hear their conversation, but she felt sure it was something her mother didn't want shared.

The trail became flatter as they wound their way around the tall cane stalks. They followed the trail, an ancient buffalo trace, for the better part of the day until they saw their Promised Land—the cabins of Fort Boone.

Boonesborough was paltry in comparison to Culpeper, with its large stone and wood homes. Despite the presence of wolves following them throughout the journey and the usual mishaps of broken bones and near drownings, the band of settlers had reached their destination.

It was a cold and dreary thirtieth of November, and news of the war with King George and the British army had reached Boonesborough. Maggie had overheard her parents talking of the number of Tories in the group. Jacob was a member of the local militia at home, and he would be expected to protect the colony of Kentucke from the British, as he had the colony of Virginia. The likelihood of a confrontation with the British seemed less troublesome than a surprise attack by the Indians.

The families that arrived from the Boone and Bryan family cabins in North Carolina began hugging their relatives and telling of their adventures since leaving the settlement.

Those who had been at the fort since May of 1775, upwards of thirty, had been inside their cabins and opened the doors to see who'd arrived. Jacob surveyed their appearance. It was a hard life, for sure, but they were surviving and making Kentucke their home.

All the way to the bank of the Kentucke River were massive oak, chestnut, and hickory trees. Cardinal birds flitted from tree to tree, chirping the arrival of newcomers. Stumps protruded from the cold and snowy ground, the remains of the ax and fro that cleared them for cabins and outbuildings. Maggie and Will were amazed at the size of the trees. One large elm tree caught their eyes. The girth was as big as a log cabin.

Rebecca Boone called for her daughter, fifteen-year-old Susannah, who was married and now expecting her first child, to come out of her cabin. Maggie watched as the pretty young girl emerged, running to embrace her father and mother. Her siblings clung to her as if they were hanging on to her for life and limb. It was a joyous reunion for the Boone and Bryan families. The Callaways and Hendersons were also greeting their relatives. They were a close clan of families, their kin married into the other's family.

Mary Katherine and Maggie watched as the families hugged and kissed their relatives.

"I miss my family back home in Culpeper," Maggie shared. She thought of the large Christmas gathering they would miss this year.

"We have no family back home in Philadelphia. My Pa came from Scotland when he was seventeen. I wish I could go there." Mary Katherine's Scottish brogue was softer than that of her father.

The men walked to an area where there were no cabins. It was there they would build their temporary family shelters.

After a pot of bear stew was shared with the new arrivals, everyone began the task of unpacking their axes and cooking wares. There was no time to waste on visiting or lollygagging. Soon there would be heavy snows and ice to blanket the fort and surrounding cabins.

Maggie felt a chill course through her body. She pulled her wool blanket around her and helped drag the pine boughs her father had cut to make the roof of their lean-to. By nightfall, the shelters would be ready.

The Diele family had traveled two months and a half to reach Kentucke, and on this night, Jacob prayed for protection in this new land.

Chapter 8

May 9th, 1776

Maggie celebrated her thirteenth birthday with a blackberry pie. Christena had saved the last of the sugar before leaving Culpeper for a special occasion. She baked the pie over the coals in the open fireplace inside the cabin. Jacob fashioned a fireplace like the one Mr. Anderson built in his blockhouse.

Christena made the small cabin as homey as possible. The fine puncheon floor replaced the hard dirt floor a few days ago. The four walls of the cabin were chinked tight and the pegs that Jacob inserted were used to hang items to keep the cabin free of clutter. A rope bed in the corner was the latest work of Jacob's master craftsmanship.

The table in the center of the room was made of fine hickory. Will had helped his father rub the wood with oil cloth to give it the dark color. On the mantle sat the china cup and saucer Christena protected on the journey. She was proud to have such finery in the wilderness.

Her spinning wheel sat proud against the wall opposite the door. She had argued with Jacob about gifting the wheel to her sister, now she was thankful for the battle. She'd already taught Maggie how to use it.

Next to the fireplace, sat the butter churn and a small stool. The brindle heifer, Ursula, gave fresh milk for the family and some would be churned into creamy butter.

Jacob made Lydia's baby boy, Brody, a cradle from the leftover hickory wood. It was a fine gift. Everyone was happy settling into their new homes.

On this day, Maggie's birthday, a blue jay scolded her pup, a hound from the litter of Mrs. Squire Boone. Jane Boone had brought the female hound all the way from North Carolina. The pups all died but one, this one Maggie raised from a small mite. She named him Tracker because he followed Maggie's every step. She'd managed to bring him inside, against her mother's protests. She promised to make him a good watch dog. Christena relented with her bribe. A good watch dog was a blessing.

She rapped on the McCampbell's door. Lydia McCampbell came to the door holding Brody on her hip.

"Good morning, Mrs. McCampbell," Maggie chirped.

"Tis a fine morning, darlin', it bein' yer birthday." Lydia moved aside, allowing Maggie to enter the dark cabin. The cabin was sparse in comparison to the Diele's.

Mary Katherine entered the cabin from her chore of fetching wood for the fire.

"Happy birthday, Maggie." Mary Katherine gave her friend a hug. "I made something for you." She went over to her bed and retrieved a small handkerchief of the finest ecru muslin. Mary Katherine had embroidered Maggie's initials, AMD, on the corner.

Maggie turned the gift over, admiring the stiches. A broad grin covered her face.

"Oh, Mary Katherine, it's beautiful! I will treasure it always."

"Mother, may I walk with Maggie?" She looked to her mother, who was nursing her baby brother in one of the cane-bottom chairs beside the fireplace.

"I suppose it 'twouldn't do any harm. I'll be needin' yer help to gather the eggs and weed the garden patch. Go along and don't stray away."

The girls closed the door and turned toward Maggie's cabin, but a commotion at the end of the fort caught their attention.

Nathan Reid, a young Virginian who'd rode into the settlement earlier in the month with Captain Floyd, had been followed by two Shawnee through the cane brake. His horse bolted before the two Indians reached him.

"He's fair to look upon, don't you think, Maggie?" Mary Katherine's eyes feasted upon the young officer.

Maggie felt Tracker thumping his tail against her. She bent down to pat his head.

Maggie and Mary Katherine watched as Jemima held his attention. Fanny Callaway and her sister, Betsy, joined the party of two.

"The Callaway girls have their share of admirers here, too. Betsy is intended to Samuel Henderson," Maggie said.

"I've noticed Israel Boone looking your way." Mary Katherine gave a teasing pinch on Maggie's cheek.

"You talk nonsense. Levina Boone and I have exchanged pleasantries, but nothing with her fair-haired brother." Maggie appeared nonplus as she scratched Tracker's fat belly.

In the distance, the loud booms of musket fire startled the girls from their conversation. A flurry of activity buzzed around them as the men hurried to retrieve their firearms and the women rushed to secure their cabins. Both Christena Diele and Lydia McCampbell instructed their children to return to their respective cabins.

"Indians!" Maggie gasped. She squeezed Mary Katherine's hand and the two parted.

The other cabin doors shut, and windows were bolted as Maggie hurried past to the safety of her mother's arms.

"Where's Will?" Christena held Maggie close.

"He was down by the river with the Grundy boys." Maggie felt her mother's fear pass through her arms to Maggie's shaking body.

In a flash, Christena was standing outside of the cabin. Jacob ran past her, having been hunting away from the settlement with Evan McCampbell and Thomas Grundy. The Grundy's slave, Lazarus, carried the large rabbit and two squirrels from the hunt.

"Jacob, go bring Will back. He's down by the river." Christena's voice cracked with fear.

Jacob stopped for a moment, loading Old Nell. The other men did the same, seeing the panic within the settlement.

The sound of Indian war whoops came from beyond the settlement. Daniel Boone, along with his brother, Squire, and the young men, Flanders Callaway and Nathan Reid, mounted their horses and took off in the direction of the commotion.

Jacob hurried past them, yelling that his son and the Grundy boys were alone by the woods. A look of disdain washed over Captain Boone's face. He didn't take the time to reprimand Jacob or comment on their predicament. He smacked his horse's rear and rode off.

The boys, oblivious to their situation until hearing the fearful sounds across the river, ran for their lives, up the path to the cabins. From the cane brake came a lone Indian, covered in red and black paint, his cropped hair spiked atop his head.

He raised his war club in the air as his horse advanced on the three boys.

"Wilhelm!" Jacob screamed, his hands shaking as he aimed Old Nell for the Mingo Indian.

A chorus of shots rang out and the black powder clouded the view Jacob had of his son. The Indian's war club had found its target. Josiah Grundy lay motionless on the ground, bleeding from the gaping wound to his skull. His brother, Anson, had tried to use his slingshot but couldn't get the volley off before the Indian fell to the ground. It was unclear who took down the Indian, as Jacob and Evan McCampbell fired together. Thomas Grundy reached his youngest son, seeing the severity of his wound.

"Get to the cabin, Wilhelm, and don't stop until you are safe inside," Jacob commanded. He continued to the spot where the Indian lay crumpled on the ground. He picked up the war club, covered with the blood of Josiah Grundy. He took the tomahawk that was fastened with a sinew cord around the Indian's waist.

Thomas scooped his son into his arms and ran for the cabin, telling his oldest son Anson, to follow.

Lazarus ran ahead to alert Mrs. Grundy of her son's misfortune. She bolted from the cabin to see her young one bleeding and limp as a wet rag in her husband's arms.

"Oh, Lord help us!" she cried.

"Clear off the table, Polly," Thomas barked.

The slave girl moved the pewter plates from the table and threw a coverlet across it.

Thomas placed his son on the table as Abigail tried to stop the flow of blood with her clean apron.

"His skull, it's . . ." The blood drained from her face.

"I tried to shoot the savage before he could get his club raised." He smoothed the boy's dark hair, now wet with blood, from his face. The color of his face was becoming chalky.

Polly cowered in the corner, afraid of the gruesome site. Anson held on to his brother's lifeless hand. With no physician in the settlement, it was left to the mothers to offer what doctoring could be found.

Abigail drew in a long breath. Seeing her son's skull broken apart, there was nothing she or anyone could do. She lovingly wrapped a clean rag around the boy's head, the blood staining it and running onto the dirt floor in a continuous drip. Josiah's face had begun to swell, his eyes swollen shut.

Rebecca Boone rapped on the cabin door, bringing with her scraps of clean cloth. Hearing the extent of his injury, she knew his time was short. She recalled the attack on her beloved James. At least the boy's mother and father were there to watch him slip into the arms of Jesus.

"Mrs. Grundy, I've brought some clean bandages for your boy," Rebecca said. She saw the look of death on the boy's face. The offering came too late.

Chapter 9

Jacob returned to the cabin, his face telling the news before his lips uttered the words. Will hadn't spoke a word since the attack. He'd buried his head in Christena's lap and cried.

Maggie searched her father's eyes for a good word about young Josiah Grundy.

"The boy passed peacefully," he uttered as he dropped into the chair. "Mrs. Grundy asked if I could fashion a tight box for burying the boy. I can use what's left from the wagon." He reached for Christena's hand. The realization the coffin could've easily been for their son caused them both to weep.

This was the first time Maggie had seen her father cry. She walked over to her father and put her arms around his shoulders.

"You mustn't cry, Papa. You saved Will from the savage. Your shot brought him to the ground."

Jacob, ashamed of his moment of weakness in front of the children, wiped his eyes on the sleeve of his shirt. He still had the tomahawk in the leather pouch he carried across his chest. He'd placed the war club outside the cabin, the blood of Josiah Grundy still clinging to it.

"Will, I want you to learn to throw this tomahawk. Practice every day. It will do you better than the slingshot." He looked at the smaller musket above the fireplace. "It's time you learn how to handle the gun."

Will sniffed, using his shirt to dry the tears on his face. The decision to go off on their own had caused the death of his friend. Will had learned a hard lesson of living in the wilderness. There was an ever-present danger of Indian attacks.

"I'm sorry for going to the river, Papa. From now on, I want to kill every savage I see." Will's bravery didn't set well with his father.

"We've had enough killing for one day, son. We must never again lower our guard." Jacob handed the tomahawk to Will. He turned it over in his hand.

Maggie heard the horses riding into the fort. Her father stood, taking his musket to the door with him. He lifted the rope pull slowly. He walked out to a gathering of settlers. They had circled around the winded riders. Daniel Boone and the men who rode off an hour before tied their horses to the hitching posts.

Rebecca Boone, returning from the Grundy cabin, caught site of Daniel. She hurried to hear what he and the other men had to say.

"We followed a small band of Mingoes along the river bank up through the canebrakes. It was there we opened fire, all fell dead inside the brake. They appeared to be gathering salt down at the lick five miles back," Daniel explained.

Rebecca walked through the crowd to her husband. "The Grundy boy passed."

Her announcement was carried through the fort. Squire Boone turned to go to the Grundy cabin. The Boone's Quaker roots had influenced the younger brother of Daniel Boone into preaching the Word. His moccasined feet moved swiftly to minister to the Grundy family.

"How did the others fare?" Daniel asked.

"The Diele boy's father, Mr. Diele, took the savage down with one shot," Rebecca shared.

Jacob spoke at the mention of his son. "Wilhelm is shaken, but thanks be to God, he is safe."

"The raids are increasing throughout the wilderness. The British have given the savage's rifles to run the settlers from the Transylvania region," Flanders Callaway's voice boomed. "The fields need tending; the corn will be lost if we can't hoe the weeds from it."

"We will have to divide the men. While half are out working the fields, the rest will be on guard duty."

Daniel searched the faces of the men inside the fort. He knew the raids would increase as the Shawano, Cherokee, and Mingo worked their way down the Warrior's Path to the Yadkin Valley. They were hunting the buffalo and getting salt from the nearby licks.

As the men talked of securing the fort, Jacob went back to his cabin to hurriedly put together a burying box for Josiah Grundy. Will joined his father behind their cabin. The two began the solemn task of fashioning a crude coffin.

Maggie sat on the tick mattress in the loft. She took out the small stub of a pencil and wrote in her journal.

> *May 9th, 1776*
>
> Today I have been alive thirteen years. It is my birthday. We were visited by a savage today. Will, Josiah, and Anson Grundy were down by the river, trying to catch fish for dinner. We heard guns firing and the horrible savage war whoops. Papa, Mr. McCampbell, and Mr. Grundy came back from hunting in time to see the wicked savage club poor Josiah to death. Papa shot the Indian dead. Poor Mrs. Grundy and Mr. Grundy. Papa and Will are making a burying box for Josiah. Now there's talk of people leaving Boonesborough.
>
> Mary Katherine thinks Israel Boone noticed me. Mayhap he would if I had the looks of his

sister, Jemima. All the heads turn her way. Even yesterday, she stabbed a cane shoot into her foot, and all the boys and men hurried to her aid. I should be ashamed of my envy of her beauty. Her voice draws the boys like bees circling a honey tree.

Maggie slipped her journal under her tick mattress. She sat Elizabetha, neglected as of late, on her pillow and turned to the wall. Will settling on his pallet was the last sound she heard as she drifted off to sleep.

Chapter 10

The month of May saw the families of Boonesborough and Harrodsburg under constant fear of attack by the Indians who were upset over the influx of settlers during the year of 1776.

The war with Great Britain had taken many of the men to join the militia for the Transylvania colony. News of the battles in and around New York and Boston reached the fort in late June.

The Boone's daughter, Susannah, and her husband had welcomed their first child, Elizabeth, into the world. Christena and Maggie visited the new mother and baby.

At night, the fireflies lit up the meadow and cornfields. The corn needed tending during the day and Jacob and Will worked alongside the other men of Boonesborough to keep the raccoons, deer, and ever-present weeds from claiming the harvest.

Each day, the sentries watching over the settlement kept their powder and shot close by. After the attack on Josiah Grundy, the residents of Boonesborough kept their rifles and muskets primed and ready.

July's heat brought with it a fever that affected several families. Brody McCampbell was the first to show signs of it, worrying his parents until they too were afflicted. Christena and Abigail Grundy took turns bathing the family in cool rags to provide a small measure of comfort.

The poultices Maggie, Will, and their parents wore seemed to put a hedge of protection over them from the scourge of the fever. Thankfully, the worst of the affliction came and went without more graves being dug in the settlement.

On July 14th, Jacob read the scripture from the large Bible he'd protected all the way from Culpeper. The tall elm provided much needed shade on that sultry Sunday morning. Every now and again a breeze would lift the low hanging leaves above their heads.

Maggie listened to her father read the Fifty-first chapter of Psalms as she swatted a large horse fly that continued to harass her. Abigail Grundy's song book, brought from Williamsburg, provided the attendees with a melody few could join. Her voice carried across the fields, quieting the blue jays and sparrows sitting above them.

After the reading of the Word, everyone made their way back to their cabins for a day of rest. The young boys sat on the ground and made carvings from their whittlings while the young girls gathered under the large sycamore tree at the edge of the fort, shared secrets, and traded smiles with the young bachelors watching nearby.

Maggie and Mary Katherine were allowed on this day to be part of the crowd. Levina Boone chased after her toddler brother, Jesse, while the older girls discussed taking the canoe out for a leisurely ride down the river. Jemima thought her injured foot would benefit from the cool water.

The locust hummed incessantly from a nearby oak tree as the girls walked down to the river bank. Betsy and Fanny carried the oars while Jemima carried a small pen knife to cut wild onions for a poultice.

Maggie and Mary Katherine hurried to catch up, but upon reaching the small party were told there wasn't room in the canoe.

The younger girls watched as the dugout canoe glided quietly along. The girls' voices were soon out of earshot.

"Let's follow along the bank and see where they go. I saw Nathan Reid speaking with Jemima earlier. Mayhap they're going to meet?" Maggie pulled on Mary Katherine's arm.

"I don't see what harm could come from just following them a short distance." Her eyes darted back to the cabins.

The girls moved stealthily through the tall weeds. They watched the canoe flow through the water, an occasional splash of the paddles breaking the quiet.

The bank along the river took on a slight rise, the rocky edges protruding out and away from the trail, made it difficult for the girls to retain their stable footing. They had traveled almost a quarter of a mile when Mary Katherine halted.

"It's too far, Maggie. They've gone too far for us to stay with them."

Winded, Maggie caught her breath as she and Mary Katherine looked down the river for the carefree trio in the canoe.

The first scream jolted both girls, Maggie's heart lurched in her chest.

Did one of the girls topple into the water? Another scream, then another. The sound wasn't from splashing in the water.

"Savages! Run, Mary Katherine!" Maggie pushed the girl to move. They were too far from the settlement to yell for help.

Maggie paused to see the canoe pulled by one of the Indian captors to the north side of the bank. She heard the piercing screams again. Mary Katherine ran like a doe through the cane brake.

From behind, a dark arm went around Maggie's neck, pulling her back into his clutches.

"Mary . . . . Maggie screamed, but a hand covered her mouth. She tried to bite and kick her captor before he twisted her around to a knife pointed at her throat.

Chapter 11

Evan McCampbell serenaded the settlement with a soothing fiddle melody. Christena churned butter to the tune. The sun's rays dipped behind the dark forest.

Screams coming from the direction of the river startled the whole fort. Daniel Boone, who'd been lying in bed, jumped for his rifle and tore from the cabin, forgetting to don his moccasins.

Another scream jolted Evan McCampbell. He looked to Lydia, sitting on a stump bouncing the baby on her knee, and both gasped at the realization it was their daughter.

"By heaven, that be Mary Katherine." His heart nearly leapt from his chest.

He ran to the cabin to get his rifle. Jacob, Thomas Grundy, Captain Floyd, Nathan Reid, and Colonel Callaway reached the river when Mary Katherine, screaming to the top of her lungs ran out of the cane, her face nearly drained of its color. Betsy Callaway's intended, Samuel Henderson, reached the water's edge when he saw the McCampbell girl dart from the cane brake, screaming at the top of her lungs.

Daniel Boone grabbed her by the shoulders, "Was it the Indians? Do they have the girls?"

Mary Katherine tried to form the words, however all that escaped her lips was another shriek.

By this time, Evan reached his daughter and pulled her into his embrace.

"You're safe, lass."

Jacob caught his breath, expecting to see Maggie coming out of the cane brake behind her.

"Where's Maggie? Is she with you?" His legs weakened like a newborn colt.

Mary Katherine turned to the path. Tears streamed down her face, her father's arm wrapped protectively around his daughter.

"We saw Fanny, Betsy, and Jemima in the canoe, then four . . . maybe . . . five savages came out of the woods. They were too close to the north shore."

Jacob, impatient, asked again, "Where is Maggie?"

"One savage got clear into the water and pulled them to the shore," she continued.

Jacob felt fear rising in his chest, causing his breath to come in short spasms.

"Was she with Jemima?"

"No, we saw them get pulled into the woods and Maggie told me to run." Mary Katherine's eyes widened, a fearful expression growing on her face. "I heard her scream, but I didn't look back. I ran."

Jacob had little time to decide. Daniel Boone and the party had decided to let Colonel Callaway pursue the girls with his horsemen toward the Lower Blue Licks and try to cut the Indians off when they tried to cross the river, while Boone would take his party along the trail in the general direction in which they were heading.

"Captain Boone, my Maggie was taken on the bluff. I'm riding back the way the McCampbell girl came from the path."

"You best take another or two with you. We'll follow the trail from across the river. If you don't find any sign when you get to the bluff, go back to the fort. She might be with the others."

"I'll ride with you, Jacob." Thomas Grundy was standing beside him, rifle loaded and ready.

Neither waited for Captain Boone's blessing. They started through the pea vine and clover. Not trained in Indian tracking, the best they could hope for was to see Maggie's hobnail heels imprinted into the soft earth.

Back at the settlement, no one knew for certain what the screams and shrieks were about, but Rebecca Boone and Jane Boone gathered up the youngest of the children and ran for the blockhouse. Every able-bodied man and boy who could load and shoot a rifle ran to the blockhouse with powder horns and guns.

Lazarus was among the men who brought the horses, mules, and cattle into the palisade.

Everyone who had been away from the fort gathering water and tending to the animals rushed inside the fort's safety.

Lydia caught sight of her husband leading Mary Katherine by the arm, his short legs making quick tracks to the blockhouse.

"Mary Katherine, where's Maggie? Was she with you?" Christena barked.

"Yes, ma'am, she was. But she pushed me and told me to run. I didn't see who grabbed her, but I heard the commotion behind me. A savage dragged her away." Mary Katherine repeated over and over her apologies.

"My poor Maggie." Christena felt the air close in, causing her head to spin. Will had grabbed his tomahawk and mother's rifle. A powder horn swayed as he ran to the blockhouse with Anson Grundy.

For two hours, women helped load rifles and carry water to the watchmen, while everyone sat crowded on the two floors of the blockhouse. Every sound caused their muscles to flinch.

After the moon began to rise, the women and their children left the blockhouse for their cabins. The watchmen were in the blockhouse and around the perimeter of the fort. Since the Diele's cabin was larger, Abigail and Anson Grundy joined Christena and Will for the long night. Christena tried to hide her panic. Both her husband and daughter were in danger of losing their lives.

"Mama, Tracker hasn't come back." Will stared at the small wooden box where the pup usually curled with a deer antler to chew.

"I know, son. Mayhap he is leading Papa and Mr. Grundy to our Maggie," she offered. Her nerves were frayed, as were those of all the families waiting for word about their daughters.

"Try to rest, Will. I'll wake you and you can spell me with the rifle."

Will's eyes widened. His mother changed her mind about him and using the rifle. Everything was different now. Until Maggie was returned safely, Christena would never feel safe.

Chapter 12

The rough hand clasped her mouth tightly, spinning Maggie around to face him. The sight of him brought another muffled scream, but the blade of the Indian's knife touched her throat, followed by a grunt. Maggie understood the body language, and she obeyed.

He quickly tied her hands with a buffalo tug and allowed her to keep her shoes. In a flash, he was pulling her down the steep bluff, the rocks tumbling to the bank below as the two hurried to reach an awaiting horse tethered to a slender willow tree.

She tried to look at her surroundings for the three girls, but she saw no other Indians. The canoe was banked where Jemima, Fanny, and Betsy were pulled ashore. The Cherokee brave, covered in grease and red paint, pushed her toward the horse.

"*A-gi-lv-di*," he said, motioning for her to mount the horse. "*Nu-li-s-dv*," His voice was more than a whisper, and it was forceful. She didn't understand his words, "Ride, quickly." He mounted the horse behind her and dug is heels into the horse's flank.

Maggie could hear the sounds coming from a different direction than what the Indian was riding. She wanted to yell for her father, she heard the voices of Jemima and Betsy, then their voices were silent. Maggie could only imagine what was happening to her friends. She remembered poor Josiah Grundy. The Indian didn't appear to be traveling with the five who took the other girls. His skin reeked of body odor and grease.

The two traveled a short distance to a salt lick near the river. It was here he decided to cross the shallows. Maggie would be too far down river for anyone to hear her, but she rolled off the horse, hitting the ground with a thud that jarred her teeth. She bit her tongue, a warm, rusty taste causing her to spit the blood onto the ground. Without care, she wiped her chin on her sleeve. The Indian jumped from the horse and jerked her to stand. She had one chance, and she yelled for her life.

"Papa! Papa!" she shouted over the ripples in the water and crows cawing in the branches above them.

Her captor shook her until her teeth rattled. *"E-lu-we-i."* Silent!

Maggie knew someone would be looking for her, but what if they didn't realize she was with a different Indian going a different direction? Her heart sank.

Surely her voice carried up the river. The Indian pushed her back onto the horse. Maggie grimaced as he tightened the buffalo tug on her wrists.

"Ni-hi a-gi-lv-di, tla ga-wo-ni-s-g!" You ride, no talking.

"I don't understand," Maggie tried to communicate with the savage.

He repeated his command, patting the blanket on the chestnut mare.

"Very well," Maggie relented. She dug her heel into the soft earth. Mayhap someone would see the indentation and know to follow across the river. She wasn't allowed to ride side-saddle as a lady, but a straddle. She felt embarrassed for her knees being bear. She settled herself, holding tight to the horse's mane.

Her captor leapt onto the horse's back. He nodded, *"O-s-dv."* Good.

The horse crossed the shallows, the water moving swiftly over the rocks. Maggie sat still as a statue, trying to hear anyone calling for her. The horse reached the bank on the other side of the river. A faint sound came through the soft breeze against their backs.

It was Jacob's voice. She recognized her name, even with the sound coming from a distance too far to see the searchers.

She started to reply, but the Indian put his hand over her mouth and hissed, "*E-lu-we-i.*" Silence.

Despair overtook Maggie. This would be her last chance, and she knew it. The Indian was taking her south, away from her family.

Jacob and Thomas followed the tracks as far as the decline to the river. There were two sets of horse tracks. Thomas suggested they were from another rider. Jacob's voice echoed through the river bottom as he called for Maggie. They hurried to the river's edge. It was there they saw hoof prints and a deep impression of a heel.

"Jacob, did Maggie have on shoes or was she barefoot?" Thomas asked, observing the heel imprint.

"She wore heels." He rose, looking across the river. "If you want to return, I won't begrudge you."

Thomas took off his cap and scratched his head. "I reckon you wouldn't leave me."

The sound of horses across the river caught them by surprise. Colonel Callaway saw the men before they saw him. "Did you see the horses cross the river?"

"No, just one set of tracks here at the edge," he shouted.

Callaway rode his horse with the other horsemen further down the bank. They saw several tracks leading up to the weeds and vines that covered the floor of the forest. He circled back to join the others waiting by the river's edge.

"Boone is going to parlay with us after tracking to the south," he kept his voice low as to not arouse any Indians still within the area.

"I'll cross here. I think the Indians were part of the same group, and Maggie is most likely with them." Jacob put his musket across his lap as he nudged his heels into the horse's side.

The water lapped against his shoes as he spurred his skittish horse through the swift current. Thomas checked the bluff for movement in the trees as he entered the water.

Once across, Jacob and Thomas followed the hunting party into the dark forest.

Chapter 13

Christena Diele joined the Boone and Callaway families in keeping their hands and minds busy while their men were out searching for the girls. Word came back to the residents via thirteen-year-old John Gass, that Boone and the search party had reached a cabin built by his uncle, William Gass, and the lot of them held up in that cabin awaiting supplies and a fresh change of clothes. John had arrived in the wee hours of the morning, having come six miles through the dark forest and crossing the river alone.

They were encouraged by the scraps of material the girls left as signs. He was insistent upon gathering the supplies and heading out in the dark to meet up with the search party before daylight.

Everyone jumped into action and within short order, young Gass was on his way into the wilderness. How he found his way to and from could only be credited to Providence alone.

With the renewed hope that Boone was on the trail of the girls and their Indian captors, a burst of renewed energy fueled the mothers and family members.

Christena and Will carried buckets of water to clean the cabin from top to bottom while Jacob and Maggie were gone. She busied herself with picking the green beans that hung on the low bushes. She taught Will a German song from childhood as they broke the beans together.

Evan McCampbell brought her one of the squirrels he'd shot. Grateful for the kind gesture, she skinned and fried the squirrel over the fire. Keeping busy worked for a short time before the gnawing worry of her daughter and husband sneaked back to rob her thoughts.

Lydia McCampbell and Mary Katherine approached the Diele's cabin. Mary Katherine had spent a fitful night, worried the savage would return for her and kill the whole settlement. She spent the better part of the day inside the cabin, afraid to leave her pallet.

After news spread that the search party was on the trail of the captors, she was persuaded to leave her self-imposed lair. With gentle coaxing, she agreed to visit Mrs. Diele, Mrs. Boone, and Mrs. Callaway.

Christena smiled at her friend. Lydia toted her baby on her hip and held Mary Katherine's hand.

"Mornin', Christena." Lydia let go of her daughter's hand to push away a fallen lock of hair from her cap. She felt blessed that her daughter had been spared. She offered prayers for Maggie's safe return.

"Can you sit a spell, Lydia?" Christena looked up at Mary Katherine, who still hadn't made eye contact with her yet. "Mary Katherine, you ought not be feelin' the blame for our girls being out there." She stood from her seat to pull Mary Katherine to her breast. "I don't bear you any ill feelings for running away. You were very brave."

Hearing Christena's soft reassuring voice, Mary Katherine was like a pile of rags against her. "It's going to be alright, you'll see. Dry your eyes now."

"Yes, ma'am," Mary Katherine said.

"We're prayin' for your Maggie and the others." Lydia shifted Brody to her other hip. "If we can do anything . . ."

"Jacob will be returning soon with our girl." Christena went back to snapping beans. Her eyes met Mary Katherine's. "You'll see, they'll bring back my Maggie."

The afternoon turned to evening. The residents of Boonesborough went on about their daily routines with an apprehension as heavy as the mountain fog after a rain. Will and Anson Grundy carried water to the blockhouse for the men keeping watch. Abigail Grundy, a nervous woman having Thomas away with the search party, worsened her condition. Polly, her slave, churned butter, humming a tune as she worked. Abigail lit a pine knot to illuminate the room.

"Polly, stop humming." Abigail walked to the door. She heard the call of a wolf in the distance. "I hope Mr. Grundy returns soon." The rope and block handle moved, her eyes centered on the dark figure stepping inside.

Lazarus carried in an armful of wood for the fire. "Miz Abigail, I heerd a wolf out by the corral."

"Go tell Mr. McCampbell, and be quick," she commanded.

Chapter 14

The first night away from Boonesborough, Maggie was tied to a small sapling tree. The buffalo tug went around her upper arms and across her chest holding her fast to the tree. She tried staying awake, in case the opportunity arose for her to escape. Her captor sat across from her, chewing on a strip of dried venison. Maggie's stomach growled, as she hadn't eaten since breakfast.

The Indian thrust a piece at her. *"A-gi-s-di."* Eat.

Maggie's arms were too tightly bound for her to reach the strip of venison. Seeing her predicament, the Indian exhaled. He inched over and put the strip of venison in her mouth. She bit a piece off and chewed it quickly. She repeated the procedure until the strip was gone. The two sat staring at one another until both fell asleep.

It seemed Maggie had only slept moments. The Indian tugged at her arm, pulling her to her feet. *"Ga-do-gv!"* Stand!

"You're hurting me!" Maggie cried. The sleeve of her dress ripped at the shoulder as he jerked her upright.

He pushed her forward to mount the horse. In one fluid motion, he jumped onto the horse's back, reaching his arm down to lift her. Maggie shook her head and moved away from the Indian. He realized his mistake. Her arms, still tied, hindered her movement. She looked all around for the best escape route, only to have gotten a few yards before the Indian was upon her. He pulled the long knife from its sheath. Maggie felt the sharp point on her throat.

"U-lv-no-ti-s-gia-yv-wi-ya-a-ge-yv." He shook her. Crazy squaw.

"Where are you taking me? Please let me go." Maggie began to cry. She was tired, hungry, and certain she wasn't going to be reunited with the other girls.

"*E-lu-we-i,*" he hissed. Quiet.

He pulled Maggie by the buffalo tug and tied it to his horse. He led the horse as they moved through the dense forest. It was a humid morning. The mosquitos and gnats pestered Maggie constantly. The Indian persevered, oblivious to the insects. It seemed to Maggie that they didn't bother him, probably due to the bear grease he'd slathered on his body. Her throat was parched and her thirst powerful. She stopped, then the buffalo tug pinched the skin around her wrists.

Feeling the pull of the tug, he turned to see Maggie gesturing needing to have a drink. A smile washed over his face for the first time.

"*A-di-ta-s-di.*" Drink. He thrust a canteen made from a gourd at Maggie.

Her hands brought the tip of the gourd to her parched lips. The water dripped from Maggie's chin onto her chest. Seeing this, the Indian grabbed the gourd and took a long drink. He didn't offer her any more, putting the leather strap across his chest. He pulled at the buffalo tug, and Maggie followed the Indian in silence.

She tried to think about her father and the men who must be looking for her. She heard him call for her the day of her abduction . . . his voice remained in her mind. The tears flowed down her dirty cheeks. Her hair had fallen out of the braid she'd worn the day she was taken. Somewhere along the way, she'd lost her cap. She hoped it would be seen by those who were searching for her.

In truth, there were no searchers following Maggie Diele. They lost the trail miles back, thinking she was with the Boone and Callaway girls.

Lori Roberts

July 16th, 1776

On the third morning of their abduction, the three teen-age girls from Boonesborough had been the captives of Cherokee Hanging Maw, two Cherokee raiders, and three Shawnee warriors. Instead of going south, as the Cherokee warrior had taken young Maggie Diele, the party of five had taken their captive north toward the Shawnee towns across the Ohio River.

Jacob Diele and Thomas Grundy had given up their search along the southern route when they reached the river and found several horse's tracks. After crossing the river, they continued with Boone and the search party.

John Gass had returned with moccasins and supplies but was told to remain at his uncle's cabin. The fresh daylight proved profitable in finding the trail once again. The Indians were crafty in their deceitful ways, leading their horses in various directions to throw off any would-be followers. Once they had wasted precious time going in and out of the cane brake, it was decided after a long and heated discussion, that the Indians were most likely heading for the town situated on the Scioto River.

The families spent another night in trepidation for their men and daughters. What if the gamble by Daniel Boone took them farther away from the girls and into an ambush by Shawnee and Cherokee near the Licking Creek?

Boone and his search party crossed the Hinkston Fork of the Licking, seeing more impressions of the shoes of Betsy Callaway. They were on the right trail.

After crossing the Hinkston, they came onto the Great Warrior's Path, and there opened a great many buffalo roads. This area divided the Cherokee nation to the Shawnee nation. These buffalo roads led the travels to the Upper and Lower Blue Licks.

The search party reached the area where the buffalo and Indians would gather for the much-needed saltpeter in the brackish water.

After following the buffalo road nearly nine miles, they came to a slaughtered buffalo. They saw the buffalo's hump was missing, a favorite of the Indians, when roasted over a fire. The skin and carcass still oozed blood.

"They will stop close to water to cook the meat. We'll keep moving," Boone declared.

Jacob's heart nearly beat from his chest, the adrenaline rushing through his veins. The weary travelers continued ten miles from the Hinkston. Boone held up his arm to stop the party behind him. The trail abruptly ended. It was here the Indians and their captives entered the creek and followed close to the bank.

Boone knew the Indians were close, however, it was imperative to use caution and not rush upon the scene. Boone instructed that no man was to pull the trigger until he, Boone, directed them. Crossing the stream, the men divided.

Henderson, Reid, Jacob, Thomas, and a few others went downstream, while Boone, Floyd, and the rest proceeded cautiously up the creek. They traveled a short distance, a few hundred yards, when Boone and his men saw the Indians adding kindling to their fire near a small branch of the creek.

William Smith, part of Boone's party, advanced upon the Indians less than thirty yards away, and wanting to alert the rest, raised his hand to hurry the others to the spot. Before they could reach him, he raised his gun into the air and shot, missing his presumed target. Boone and Floyd now within shooting range, each got a shot off, wounding two of the Indians. Another shot was fired but missed the intended target.

Before the shooting began, the Indians were near the fire, attending to it and watching their captives. Hanging Maw had left the campsite moments before with a kettle for some water. Floyd wounded the warrior at the fire, but he got up and ran off. The other, as he ran, threw his tomahawk at the head of Betsy Callaway. Thankfully it missed his mark and hit the tree with a thud.

They dashed into the cane to escape. Seeing their captors fleeing, the girls jumped to their feet. Upon hearing the crack of the guns, Jemima exclaimed, "That's daddy!" and rushed toward the sound.

Afraid the girls would be shot by their captors under cover of the cane, Daniel Boone shouted, "Lay down!"

For a moment, the girls obeyed, but fearing they would miss the chance to escape, rose to their feet and began running.

Betsy Callaway wore a red bandana about her head, and with her dress cut off at the knees was taken for a wounded Indian by Thomas Grundy. He raised his gun like a club, about to bash it across Betsy's skull, when his arm was grabbed from behind by the large hands of Daniel Boone.

"For God's sake, don't kill her. We've traveled so far to save her from death!" Boone shouted.

Thomas Grundy, seeing his error, knelt to the ground and wept. Jacob reached his friend, kneeling on the ground beside him, while searching the area for his daughter.

"Is my girl, Maggie, with you?" he shouted over the jubilation of the three girls.

When the hugging and crying came to a halt, Jacob went to each of the girls, asking them again about Maggie.

"No, Mr. Diele. Hanging Maw and his savages only took us. Maggie wasn't with us in the canoe."

Jacob felt his knees go week. He'd spent the better part of three days following the trail of Boone's and Callaway's daughters, while his own daughter was being taken only God knew where.

A young deer was killed soon after. Three of the Indians had died from their wounds, while Hanging Maw and another had escaped without harm.

Jacob sat in silence while the girls told of their experiences. They relayed information about the Indians in the area and their plans to attack settlements in the Valley. The meal was eaten in haste and soon the girls and their rescuers were covering the trail back to area where the abductions took place.

The settlement of Boonesborough was left with a bare minimum of guns and protection. Just a mile from the fort, Nathaniel Hart's cabin and had been burned to the ground. His crops, orchard, and all his belongings, gone. He had left his home to help in the search for the girls.

Upon reaching the crossing, Boone raised his gun into the air firing a shot. The sound carried across the Kentucke River to the Fort at Boonesborough.

The sound came like Gabriel's trumpet to the awaiting families within the fort. Christena, Lydia, and Abigail were gathering eggs and returning with a pail of milk when the shot rang out.

"They're back! They have the girls!" Christena shouted.

They reached the edge of the settlement as Rebecca Boone, Jane Boone, and Elizabeth Callaway ran to the water's edge with the other wives. The scene was chaotic and joyous as mothers grabbed onto their daughters, their faces black with dirt and hair in tangles.

Christena ran through the confusion and cheers, searching for her daughter. Then she saw Jacob, his face drawn and somber. Mary Katherine buried her face in her mother's chest.

Jacob scooped a weak-kneed Christena into his arms. She looked on the back of his horse, assuming her child's body was thrown over the horse's back.

"Where?" she croaked, her throat tight from sobbing.

"We searched and lost the tracks. We joined with Boone and his party, thinking she was with the others." Jacob closed his eyes, desperation drained his face of color. "She's out there, and I've no idea where."

Will heard his father's words, and they stung like a hornet. "Let's go, Pa. Let me take the rifle and we'll track those bloody savages down. We gotta find Maggie."

He wiped his tears as quick as they rolled out of his eyes. Maggie would tell him not to cry.

Daniel Boone moved through the celebrating families to the Diele's.

"Mrs. Diele, I'll forever be beholden to Jacob and the men for their help in bringing back my girl." He took her hand in his. "It pains me to say we may not find your daughter."

Jacob pulled Christena to his side. "Captain Boone, I'm leaving first light. I don't expect you to leave your family now that you have your daughter."

"Jacob, I'll ride with you one day out. I don't think the Indian took her the same path as Hanging Maw took our girls. I reckon they took the southern route."

"Go celebrate with your wife and young'ins, Captain Boone. I'd be feeling better with you keeping the settlement protected." Jacob nodded toward Rebecca and Jemima surrounded by his other children and grandchild.

Jacob, Christena, and Will walked up the path to their cabin, closing the door to the whoops and hollers. Jacob placed Old Nell over the fireplace. His shoulders sagged as he put his head on his crossed arms and wept.

Chapter 15

aggie and the Indian traveled south of the Holston River on the fourth day of her captivity. The two moved swiftly through cane brakes and streams, finally stopping for food. Maggie ate nuts, berries and venison jerky, but her stomach growled for her mother's venison stew. She asked the Indian questions all the time. At one point, he put his fingers in his ears and shouted, "*A-le-wi-s-do-diga-wo-ni-s-gv!*" Stop speaking!

Maggie understood his meaning and mocked him. He turned on his heels, thinking of chucking her for being disrespectful. She stood her ground, something she'd worked up the courage to do.

The morning of the fifth day, Maggie noticed the mountains looming before her. She was tired, and her swollen feet bled from the blisters that had formed and rubbed raw.

Her captor went to the deerskin pouch thrown across the horse and produced a pair of moccasins.

"*A-nu-wo-s-di.*" Wear.

Maggie understood the meaning. She reached for the soft moccasins, smiling at the gesture. "Thank you."

The Indian nodded. Did he understand English? She pulled off her shoes and replaced them with the gifted moccasins. She wiggled her toes, the soft hide already felt wonderful. Why did white people have to wear stiff shoes when these were more comfortable?

They followed a swift moving stream to the south. Maggie had watched the sun's shadow, it was something Israel

Boone had taught her and Will back home at Boonesborough. The day was already hot. Her stomach growled loud enough for her captor to hear it. He was hungry as well but chose not to stop. Instead, he produced more of the dried jerky. The two ate in silence.

She felt the pang of homesickness stab her at the thought of her family. They must be out of their minds with worry. Mayhap they had given her up for dead? Maggie wanted her mother—to hear her call her *poppet* and hold her tight. She thought about Elizabetha and wished she'd brought her along.

They continued riding along the buffalo trail. The woods were full of deer and small game. At night, the wolves came near the campfire, but didn't venture into the fire's light. She went to sleep thinking of her mother's face and her father's voice as he read from the big Bible each night. On this night, she prayed for her family. She prayed for Captain Boone and her father to rescue her and take her back to Boonesborough.

Christena grew more melancholy with each passing day. She guarded Will's every step and forbade him from wandering away from the fort. He had nightmares each night after Josiah Grundy's death, and his sister's abduction added to his anxiety.

On July 21st, Jacob Diele gathered food, powder, and cartridges for Old Nell. Will awoke as his father added the provisions to his pack.

"Papa, can I go with you to fetch Maggie back?" He yawned.

Knowing the dangers of leaving the protection of the fort weighed heavily on Jacob's mind.

"Will, I need you to stay and protect your Mama. You can shoot your rifle now, and she needs your help around the cabin." He rubbed Will's unruly hair.

"I'll take care of Mama, Papa." Will's shoulders straightened with the new responsibility.

Christena and Jacob walked to the hitching post where Saul waited for its rider. She nuzzled against his soft hunting shirt. "Come back to me with your hair and our Maggie. God go with you." She disregarded propriety and kissed him square on the lips.

Jacob promised to watch for arrow and club, taking Old Nell from Christena. Thomas Grundy and Evan McCampbell came from the corral with their horses.

"If ye be goin' to find yer Maggie, we be a'goin with ye." Evan took his place atop his horse.

Lazarus held the reins of Thomas's horse as he situated himself in the saddle.

Jacob surveyed the men with their powder horns and rifles. Not taking Captain Boone or his more experienced woodsmen could prove disastrous for the trio. With two extra horses in tow, the men rode to the spot where Mary Katherine emerged from her narrow escape. Jacob nudged his horse forward.

Daniel Boone's offer to join Jacob hadn't escaped the earshot of some of the men because five of the men who'd returned from the search party mounted their horses and joined the trio. They rode the buffalo trail to the Blue Lick. Once they reached the place where the party forded the river in search of the Boone and Callaway girls, they followed the trail north in hopes they'd pick up the trail from there. The girls overheard the Indians talking about going to their villages north of the Ohio River. Mayhap Maggie's captor took her to a Shawnee village.

On the morning of the sixth day, they lost the trail. The men rode until there were no tracks to follow. Jacob felt the desperation overtake him.

"I don't expect any of you to continue searching. It appears futile to keep going when we aren't even sure the Indian took my girl north." He wiped his face with the sleeve of his shirt. "God be with her now and forever."

"Come, let's turn for Boonesborough," Thomas said, nudging his horse.

The men followed Thomas Grundy, riding with their rifles on the ready. Each kept their eyes alert to any movement off the trail.

Jacob's heart sank lower with each mile the horses carried them away from the Blue Licks. How would he walk into the cabin without Maggie?

Christena saw Tracker's ears perk up as the men came riding up from the riverbank. She stopped churning the butter. "They're back!" she said, looking at Will who sat whittling a whistle from a piece of a hickory branch.

Christena's heart thumped against her chest as she ran down the dirt path to the river. She searched the riders for Maggie, each one bearing only the solemn face of the searcher.

"Where's Maggie?" she asked as the men rode past her, shaking their heads. Jacob was the last to come out of the cane break.

"Jacob . . ." she managed to say, her throat squeezed tight with fear.

"Papa, where's Maggie?" Will and Tracker ran past a weary Jacob, peering down the path.

"We searched as far as the tracks were visible. We went further than safety allowed. We found the trail went cold." He grabbed Christena to him, holding her tight. Her knees failed to hold her upright.

"No . . . not my poppet," Christena wailed.

"Papa, mayhap you went the wrong way?" Will's tears mingled with smudges of dirt as he wiped his face.

"I don't know, son. The Indians travel the Warrior's Road to the villages north. They could have gone that route, but we saw signs of the horse going south." He led Saul to the corral.

"My poor poppet. I can't bear the thought of the torture . . . her last moments on this earth," Christena wailed, her heart feeling as if it were being pulled from her chest.

The women from the settlement heard from their men of the lost trail. Abigail Grundy was first to reach her friend.

"I made you a cup of sassafras tea. Come inside and wash your face, Tena."

"Thank you," she said, her voice barely audible.

"I hate the savages. I want to kill them all," Will shouted. He went inside the cabin and produced the Indian toma-hawk.

"Why did we ever leave Culpeper for this God-forsaken land? It's stained with blood. The blood of our children." Christena turned to Jacob.

"We shouldn't have left Culpeper. It's my fault our Maggie is gone." Jacob walked inside the cabin, his heart broken at the thought his daughter wasn't coming home.

Chapter 16

August 15, 1776

A dog ran to meet the Indian and Maggie, barking first, then running in circles around the horse. Maggie thought of her own pup, Tracker. He was only a pup, but mayhap he could pick up her scent if allowed to join a search. Maggie lost track of the days she and the Indian had been traveling. She'd been gone almost 4 weeks.

"*A-su-la-go-i-s-di, gi-tli,*" Hush, dog!

The dog scampered away, understanding the Indian's meaning. Maggie tensed when she saw the Indian's village. Did he bring her here, so they could torture and kill her?

He led the horse into the crowd that gathered around him and his captive. Several of the males touched her long tresses, rubbing their fingers through it. Maggie pulled back, bringing about jeers and whoops from the crowd.

Maggie held tight to the reins of the horse. The village was nestled into an area larger than Boonesborough. There were dwellings that resembled upside down baskets. The homes were made of wattle and daub—a dwelling constructed from a frame of wood, river cane and vines, and then coated with plaster made from earth and clay. The roof was made from wood or thatched grass. She expected there were at least 30 of the dwellings. It seemed the whole village stopped what they were doing to encircle the young Indian man and Maggie Diele.

"*A-gi-s-di-yi e-la-di.*" Get down. His gesture prompted Maggie to slide off the horse. He led her by the buffalo tug through the crowd. They pawed and pushed her as she tried to avoid their hands. The children stared at her with wide eyes.

Maggie didn't speak, her throat ached from holding in her despair. Tears tumbled from her eyes as she imagined the horrors that awaited her.

The Indian pulled the buffalo tug closer to him. A woman wearing a long dress made of doe skin exchanged words with the Indian, looking at Maggie, continuing their conversation.

Maggie's eyes darted to another woman standing outside of her cabin, her hair tangled and unkempt. She heard something, the sound drew her from the threshold of the cabin.

A group of children joined in the crowd, their dark eyes watching her every move. They laughed and pointed at her, and Maggie wondered what she must look like after being away from a brush or washing tub for almost a month. She swiped the hair away from her face, raising her head in defiance.

The Indian yanked the rope, causing her moment of confidence to disappear into embarrassment. She stumbled, inciting a chorus of jeers and cheers from the children and adults. The woman who'd been talking to Maggie's Indian captor gave a stern look to the children, and their behavior corrected. She called again for the woman at the cabin to come to her. Maggie couldn't make out what the Indians were saying, but she surmised from the short command it was the woman's name.

"*U-s-diA-li-so-qua-lv-di,*" she said. Little Bear "*Ni-hiu-we-tsi-a-ge-yvv-le-ni-do-hvu-hana-quua-tle-a-s-di-yi.*"   Your daughter's life is avenged.

Little Bear understood. Her eyes surveyed Maggie from head to foot. No longer did her eyes hold sorrow. She nodded to the captor, as if to agree.

The woman, named Nanye'hi, was a Ghi-ga-u, Beloved Woman, to the Cherokee. Her son, Hi-s-gi-di-hi, Five Killer Kingfisher, was Maggie's captor.

Chapter 17

Maggie was presented to Nanye'hi by her son. Upon closer inspection, she wasn't much older than Christena Diele. Her dark eyes were like twin inkwells. She wore her black hair in a long braid down her back. She wasn't much taller than Maggie, but her proud posture gave the appearance of a woman much taller.

She listened to her son, Hi-s-gi-di-hi, Five Killer. He explained coming back from a raiding party with three other Shawnee braves who were killed by the settlers during a raid at Boonesborough. He told one of the Shawnees killed a young boy, and he spotted the Callaway and Boone girls being taken by the Hanging Maw and other Cherokee. He chose his captive to avenge the death of Little Bear's daughter, A-tsi-lv-s-gv. She had been killed the previous year as a group of settlers came to Kentucke after the Sycamore Shoals conference. Little Bear's husband, Amo-adawehi, was killed near the Kentucke River on a raiding party after their daughter's death. Her mourning period for her husband and daughter was ending. She took the buffalo tug and yanked Maggie away from Five Killer. Maggie's eyes popped open. At least Five Killer hadn't harmed her.

Little Bear pulled Maggie toward her cabin, speaking softly to her. The last year had been lonely for the young squaw. Maggie had belonged to Five Killer. He was the one who took her. He chose to present Maggie to his mother. Nanye'hi had two daughters with her Scots-Irish husband, Bryant Ward. She gave Maggie to Little Bear to ease her pain.

"Oww," Maggie yelled as she stepped on a sliver of deer antler that poked through her moccasin. She wondered why the Indian gave her to this woman.

Little Bear looked over her shoulder and saw the deerskin moccasins on Maggie's feet. Her eyes took on a look of sadness, thinking of her own daughter who would have been the same age as Maggie.

Maggie walked obediently behind Little Bear, into the dark and smoky cabin. Her eyes adjusted to the darkness and her present situation.

A shadow appeared in the doorway before Little Bear could close it. Nanye'hi came into the cabin, speaking first to Little Bear in a soft voice. Maggie listened to the strange language, her ears strained to make out a familiar word or phrase. The conversation turned to Maggie.

"You belong to Little Bear now. Do as she tells you."

Maggie's heart leaped in her chest. This woman spoke English. The words hadn't sunk in.

"My name is Maggie." She looked at Little Bear, her face stern and unmoved.

"You will have Cherokee name. You are Little Bear's to name as she wishes." Nanye'hi turned to Little Bear and spoke the words in Cherokee. Her countenance softened, and she embraced Nanye'hi. Maggie crouched on the floor, her legs feeling like those of a newborn colt. After more discussion, the women moved across the room to where Maggie was, holding her knees to her chest.

"Stand, young one," Nanye'hi said. She waited for Maggie to comply.

A look of compassion washed over Little Bear's face. She patted her chest and said, "*U-ni-tsi.*" Mother.

She pointed to Maggie, "*Ahyoka.*"

Nanye'hi spoke in English, "You are now Cherokee. You will be Ahyoka, it means 'she brought happiness'."

At first, Maggie didn't understand what had transpired between the two women. Her realization that she belonged to Little Bear as her daughter caused Maggie to cry for her mother and father. She had been gone for twenty-eight days, and in her heart, she knew she would never see them again.

Little Bear and two squaws led Maggie down a path to the creek. Her clothing, now dirty and torn, was removed. She refused to remove her shift. The women rebuked her, and Maggie was forced to comply. The water was cold, but oddly she welcomed the coolness on her sunburnt cheeks. The women dunked her into the water, which she protested by waving her arms about. Her shoulder length brown hair was washed, and her body scrubbed clean. The bath washed away her fears, the women meant her no harm.

The squaws chatted happily with Little Bear. One of the women, Inola, carried a bear skin robe to wrap around Maggie as she exited the creek. Woya presented Maggie a soft doeskin dress with fringe at the arms and bottom. The moccasins Five Killer had given her earlier were replaced with a pair of the softest deerskin with intricate beaded designs across their tops.

Her shift was thrown in a pile with the rest of her clothes. For modesty, a breechcloth, similar to the warrior's attire, was handed to Maggie to put on under the dress. She slipped the dress over her head. The soft buckskin glided over her arms and fell to her ankles.

Maggie remembered her manners. "Thank you," she said, to each of the women. They listened, then repeated in Cherokee, "*Wado*."

They nodded in approval when Maggie echoed, "*Wado.*" The squaws set to brushing her long tresses with a porcupine quill brush. Little Bear handed Maggie a curious beaded leather pouch. She put it around her neck. It made her think of her journal. A sprig of sage was tucked inside. "Thank . . ." Maggie repeated the Indian's word, "*Wado.*"

"*U-we-tsi-a-ge-yv,*" Little Bear said. Daughter.

Maggie smiled, not understanding Little Bear's words. She repeated, "*Wado.*"

That evening, Nanye'hi, the Beloved Woman, introduced Maggie to the council as Ahyoka. Maggie was brought to the large building in her new regalia and moccasins. She followed Nanye'hi and Little Bear through the doorway. The room was semi-dark, and it appeared there were different groupings among the Indians. She didn't realize the assembly was sitting according to their clan.

The Council House was larger than any building in Boonesborough. It rivaled in size to the German Lutheran Church back home in Culpeper where she and her family worshipped.

The house was built in a circular shape, with perpendicular walls eight feet high ending at a point, giving the roof a conical form. The building was supported by interior posts.

From the floor to the highest point of the roof measured fifteen to twenty feet. Puncheons were placed around on the inside to serve as seats. The house was covered with the bark of hickory shrubs, or white oak shreds. A doorway was visible, and on the outside, a small shed was attached. In front of this, a level yard laid off in a square, was kept smooth for dancing.

Maggie felt her heart pounding in her ears. She listened as Nanye'hi spoke to the Chief, his dark hair plucked from his head, save for a center lock that was painted red. His face gave Maggie chills. Red and black lines were painted on his face, and from his nose was a curious metal disc. His ears were pierced with small discs hanging from them.

The women sat in the council. Maggie strained to hear all that was said, but no one spoke in broken English. She tried recognizing words by their gestures, but her head started to ache from concentrating so hard. The Beloved Woman spoke to the chief, their words too low for Maggie to hear. The warriors raised their voices in agreement with the chief. How Maggie wished she could understand the conversations going on around her.

As terrifying as Five Killer was to Maggie at the time of the killing of Josiah Grundy and her captivity, she received compassion and acceptance as an adopted daughter of Little Bear.

For the first time since her capture, she ate a simple meal of potatoes, corn cake, and a chunk of dried venison.

She didn't understand the language spoken around her, however, she watched their hand signs and soon began to understand their meaning. No one addressed her by her real name. She wished someone would talk to her.

She thought of her mother. It was dinner time at Boonesborough. She would be helping her mother set the table. Will, oh, how she missed her brother! He would be taking his turn at helping lead the stock to the river. Her father, after dinner, would light the pine knot to read from the big Bible.

She wondered if the Indians were heathens, as she'd heard Abigail Grundy say. No one offered a prayer before eating.

Maggie's heart was heavy. How would she ever be happy? Her name was all that she brought with her to this place. And now, they had taken that away.

Chapter 18

aggie lay on a bed of straw covered with soft rabbit pelts, sewn together. It was as if she were lying on a cloud. She was inches away from Little Bear, who fell asleep as soon as the candle was extinguished. She listened to a chorus of crickets outside the small dwelling.

Her heart ached for the soft touch of her mother's hand on her cheek when she kissed her goodnight. Maggie thought of her doll, Elizabetha. It didn't seem to matter now if she was too old to play with her. Now it was something for her mother to have to remember her. She felt the warm trail of a tear roll down her face.

She thought about the Callaway girls and Jemima Boone. What had become of them? She thought of her puppy, Tracker. She was glad he hadn't followed her that day. She was sure Five Killer would've slain him rather than let him bark and lead a search party to them.

Maggie couldn't keep the tears from rolling down her cheeks. She tried to muffle the sound by burying her face into the blanket roll she used as a pillow.

Little Bear raised her head and looked over to where Maggie lay. She turned to the wall, falling back to sleep.

Maggie tried to keep track of days, but soon one day blended into the next. She lost count sometime after thirty. It must be mid to late August. Five Killer and other warriors had left soon after Maggie arrived at the village. Her heart still ached for her parents and brother. She missed Mary Katherine and their talks about boys.

She began to comprehend some of the words Little Bear spoke to her.

Little Bear pounded her chest and said, "*U-ni-tsi.*" Mother.

Maggie nodded, she understood her meaning.

Little Bear's smile showed her approval of Maggie. Five Killer's gift was good medicine for her soul. Little Bear, no matter how kind, would never take the place of Maggie's mother. She guarded her heart. No matter what her Indian captors called her, she would always be Maggie Diele.

Every day since coming to the village, she watched the stockade doors and listened for the dogs to bark, signaling an intruder. At first, Little Bear stayed close to Maggie. The only time she escaped the watchful eyes of her Indian mother was after she lay on the pallet at night. At night, she lay awake thinking how she could escape, foolish as it was.

Will anyone come after me?

Maggie spent most of her day with two girls who were near her age. They taught her to play Chunkey, a game that used a smooth stone disk and two slender poles. She watched for days as the girls played. One day she joined as did Little Bear and the two squaws who were with her on the day she was presented to the council.

Maggie laughed when Tayanita whacked Galilani in the shin with the pole. It felt good to laugh, even if her heart was sad. The difficulty in communicating with the clan in which she belonged was frustrating. She understood simple commands through hand gestures by Little Bear and her friends, Tayanita and Galilani. The looks she received when she spoke in English were silent admonitions, it made her use Cherokee if she wished to be included in conversations. She knew the Beloved Woman could converse with her in English, but she didn't.

She didn't understand the conversations of the young girls, and no one spoke English to her.

Chapter 19

The month of August came and went. With the month of September, Maggie's captivity entered its second month. The forest turned from lush green to a cornucopia of bright orange, yellow, and red. The squirrels scampered throughout the camp gathering the nuts below the massive oak trees.

Maggie awoke from her pallet of skins, noticing Little Bear had left the structure. She quickly dressed and went outside. The smell of bear meat cooking on the fire filled her nostrils. Her stomach growled in reaction to the delicious smell rising from the fire.

Maggie saw Bryant Ward, Nanye'hi's white husband. He entered the village riding a chestnut-colored horse. He spoke with an accent similar to Evan McCampbell. Maggie was shocked to see Nanye'hi embrace her husband. She wondered if he, too, was once a captive.

The village was missing several of the warriors. Five Killer had left earlier in the week with several others. Maggie didn't know where they went, but she watched as they applied fresh black and red paint to their faces and took part in a special meeting at the Council House. How she wished she could understand their words. Her palms were like two wet rags as she watched them with their war clubs and tomahawks raised over and over.

It was best she didn't know the settlement of Boonesborough was one of the targets. The belief that the men of the settlement were looking for her kept her fears at bay.

The gathering ended sometime after midnight. Maggie's eyes drooped several times, before popping open in a startled glare when the whoops and shrill yells from the women snapped her to attention.

When the Council House was emptied of the seven clans, Maggie and Little Bear entered their dwelling and fell fast asleep.

The days since Maggie's captivity were spent doing similar chores to those she'd done at Boonesborough prior to being taken by Five Killer. She joined the girls gathering potatoes from the garden. The mosquitos were less bothersome on this day as the day before. The girls wore a concoction of smashed roots of the golden seal and bear fat as a means for protection from insects. They continued gathering the vegetables while Maggie sang a ditty she remembered from her days in Culpeper. The others giggled as they worked, hearing Maggie's voice raise with enthusiasm, even though they couldn't understand the words. Crows circled the garden, eyeing the rows of corn, already harvested, but the stalks remained to dry in the late summer sun. The corn stalks were to be used for various projects. The husks were saved to make dolls and other crafts.

Once their chores were finished, they carried their baskets back to the storehouse and filled the bins with the potatoes.

Maggie knew her parents and the others would be doing the same thing at their garden plot. She felt a pang of sadness as she thought about Tracker. Will would take over the care of him. She wished she had paper and pencil to write her feelings. She didn't want to forget her words now that she was expected to speak Cherokee.

The Cherokee had no paper, but Maggie used the bark of the birch trees and the small pieces of charcoal from the cooled embers to write.

The women of the village were constantly busy with food preparation and preservation. Whenever a deer was killed, the women set to work skinning the hide and butchering the animal. The strips of venison were placed into salt, when available. The meat was placed into a large stone tub, with first a layer of salt, then meat. It was covered and put into the ground and covered with another large stone.

The meat was placed on a mud brick oven and layered onto racks and left to dry over a smoldering fire. The smell made Maggie's stomach rumble from hunger.

The Cherokee ate a variety of meat when game was plentiful, but during the winter when the bear hibernated, and deer were hunted by both white and Indian, the Cherokee depended on smaller animals to eat during the colder months. Maggie helped with the butchering of a bear that was killed by Gawonii, whose name means 'He is speaking'. She felt as though she might wretch during the butchering, but the work was quick and efficient, leaving little time for her to empty the contents of her stomach as they worked.

The women set about dressing the bear while the younger children, in front of the Council House, played with a pouch of stone marbles. Maggie watched as an elder woman, Awiagina, sat in front of her summer house weaving a basket of pine needles. Her aged fingers wove the dried needles tightly to form the bottom of the basket. Greener pine needles were woven into the basket, giving it an interesting contrast.

Maggie squatted beside her. Awiagina smiled, all her teeth were almost gone, except for two on top and two on the bottom. Maggie felt a connection with Awiagina. Mayhap it was the way her eyes sparkled through the folds of skin that draped them most of the time. She reminded Maggie of her own grandmother who still lived in Culpeper.

She stopped her weaving and held out a wad of grass to Maggie.

"*Ni-hi a-de-lo-qua-s-di*," she said. You learn.

Maggie's face lit up, even though she wasn't sure what the elder woman said, she understood the gesture. She thought for a moment, answering her. "*V-v, wa-do*," Maggie's attempt to say 'yes, thank you' brought another smile from Awiagina.

Awiagina nodded. "*O-s-dv*." Good.

Maggie found the lack of communication difficult when it came to directions for basket weaving, however, she kept her eyes fixed on the woman's hands as she showed how to begin the bottom portion of the basket. Soon, Maggie had mastered the weaving technique and was weaving her own small basket.

She'd lost track of time and found the activity enjoyable. Every so often, the elder woman would stop and correct Maggie if she wasn't pulling the grass tight enough, but Maggie didn't mind her taking her hand and pulling the grass.

The hound lying next to Awiagina opened one eye, followed by an ear twitch. Maggie noticed both of his ears rose to attention and he gave a low growl upon hearing a noise, inaudible to her.

"*A-su-la-go-i-s-di*!" Hush. Maggie's admonition did little good, as the dog continued to bark, in the direction of the palisade gate. She hadn't realized how easily she'd spoken the words. It was also a surprise to Awiagina. She nodded and muttered under her breath.

The other dogs followed suit, and the women traded glances.

Maggie remembered hearing the dogs carry on in this manner when she was brought into the village with Five Killer. Would the raiding party bring another captive? She watched Awiagina and the other women.

The Indians who had remained in the village hurried to the large wooden doors. The raiding party returned with whoops and boisterous shouting. Maggie saw two of the Indians with red and black paint on their faces and bodies. The rest came riding through the gate with two scalps. Everyone gathered around the five young Indians and raised their hands in triumph.

Maggie's stomach turned at the sight of the bloody scalps. Her memory of the attack on Josiah Grundy remained fresh in her mind. How could these Indians treat her with kindness but show no mercy for other settlers?

She watched the gestures of the warriors, their actions mimicking the horrible fate awaiting their victims.

What if they attacked Boonesborough? Maggie's heart raced with fear.

Little Bear took Maggie's hand. She was expected to take part in whatever ritual was about to take place.

Everyone in the village gathered to celebrate the successful hunt and taking the scalps of settlers who were trying to raise a cabin near the salt lick three days distance away.

Nanye'hi, dressed in a white deerskin skirt and white blouse, spoke on behalf of the Wolf clan. The other six clans assembled around the Council House according to their position within the tribe. The Cherokee clanship came from one's mother; the *Anigilohi,* meaning Long Hair, *Anisahoni,* Blue, *Aniwaya,* Wolf, *Anigotegewi,* Wild Potato, *Aniawi,* Deer, *Anitsisqua,* Bird, and *Aniwodi,* Paint clans.

It is forbidden to marry within one's clan. Clan members are considered brothers and sisters.

Maggie sat with The Long Hair Clan. The Peace Chief came from this clan.

Prisoners of war, orphans of other tribes, and others with no Cherokee tribe were often adopted into this clan. Little Bear belonged to this clan.

The Blue Clan was considered the oldest. Those who were able to make special medicines for the children came from this clan.

The Wolf Clan was the largest of the clans. The War Chief came from this clan. This clan was known as protectors.

The Wild Potato Clan was known as the keepers and gatherers of the land. The wild potato was a food staple to the Cherokee.

Members of the Bird Clan were known as messengers. The belief that birds are messengers between earth and Heaven, or the People and Creator, gave the members of this clan the responsibility of caring for the birds. The eagle feathers presented at ceremonies were only allowed to be collected by members of this clan.

The members of the Paint Clan were historically known as prominent medicine people. Medicine is painted on a patient after harvesting, mixing, and performing other duties of the ceremony.

Maggie listened to Nanye'hi speak to the council about the armies of British and settlers over the mountains. Her husband, Bryant Ward, told her the current situation with the War for Independence from Great Britain. The other tribes to the South had joined the British. The tribe must decide which side they would support.

Maggie's eyes drank in her surroundings as the great deliberations continued. A log at the front of the assembly contained chiefs who were assembled during times of war. The two braves with the scalps, Chea Sequah and Tsiyi, gave impassioned speeches about the Long Rifles, the name they called the various militias forming in the settlements near Boonesborough and the Holston River.

Thankful Bryant Ward needed Nanye'hi's interpreting, Maggie was able to listen to his words and understand.

Nanye'hi, the Peace Chief, cautioned the council for going to war with the settlers.

She wanted to run to him and ask him to take her back to Boonesborough, to her parents. She knew this was not the time or place, as the Council House's reverence was like that of her church in Culpeper.

After the various clans left the Council House according to their position to the Wolf Clan's location, Maggie followed Little Bear back to their cabin. She brought in the kindling to make a fire for their dinner. The basket she made earlier sat on the table.

Little Bear turned the basket over in her hands, judging Maggie's work. "*Tso-tlv-ne-s-go ta-lu-tsa*?" You made this?

"*V-v,*" Maggie replied. Her ability to converse with Little Bear in the Cherokee language surprised them both. The handle had been the hardest part for Maggie. A feeling of accomplishment washed over her.

"*O-s-dv, u-we-tsi-a-ge-yv.*" Good, daughter.

Maggie remembered the word. Her smile faded, and she turned back to the fire. She would never be Little Bear's daughter.

Chapter 20

The embers inside the fire pit glowed a deep red. Maggie threw broken pieces of pottery into the fire. She found herself completely alone, no one sat with her or accompanied her. She heard a mourning dove call to its mate from a pine tree nearby.

Maggie's thoughts traveled back to her room in the stone house in Culpeper. The mocking bird outside her window would recite its repertoire of calls every morning. Her eyes pinched together at the memory. How she missed her life before they crossed into the wilderness.

She tossed another chunk of pottery into the fire. She didn't hear the moccasins of Oukonunaka, the grandson of Yonaguska. He held importance during the Council, but Maggie wasn't certain of his role. In fact, she thought he was one of the chiefs of the Deer clan.

"Ahyoka."

Startled by his voice, she turned to see the young brave standing beside her. Oukonunaka's voice had already started to deepen.

"*O-si-yo.*" She put down the broken pottery shard. He knelt beside her, producing a small flute in his hand.

Maggie's eyes brightened at the site of the flute. Before she was taken captive, she often joined in with her mother singing a familiar ditty or making up her own tune.

"For you." He passed the flute to Maggie.

She tried to remember the words she had heard before. "Thank you, it's beautiful."

He waited for her to say the words in Cherokee.

"*Wa-do, it is . . . u-wo-du-hi.*" Thank you, it is pretty. Maggie examined the flute.

Oukonunaka produced a larger flute. He blew into it and a haunting melody filled the air. Maggie had listened to a fife player at home in Culpeper, and a fiddle player back in Boonesborough, but nothing like this. The flute was an instrument the Indians played often, along with the drum.

Oukonunaka finished the melody and put his flute back in the pouch at his waist. His hair was plucked except for the top knot and strip from the center front to the back. It stood tall like the quill of a porcupine. He wore a breechcloth and short hunting shirt. He was only slightly taller than Maggie. He stretched out his hand to help Maggie stand. She thanked him as she stood.

Little Bear called for her to come back to the cabin. She saw a warrior standing beside her, and her flute was forgotten for the moment.

Maggie had seen the Indian with Little Bear several times, but not understanding their conversations, wasn't sure what he meant to her. Little Bear tried to speak and gesture to her, explaining that Degatoga was her husband.

Maggie understood the meaning. She smiled but didn't feel anything toward the news. She went inside the cabin, its size already small for two. The large pallet where Little Bear slept would be occupied by two. She wondered how long her husband and daughter had been gone. Even though Little Bear had been kind to Maggie, she missed the physical touch of her mother and father. She thought about Will. What had become of her family? Were they safe, or had they met a cruel fate at the hands of the warriors? She sat on her pallet and tried placing her fingers on the flute as Oukonunaka did. She closed her eyes, concentrating on making the same notes as she'd heard.

Little Bear entered the cabin as Maggie played the flute. The sound must've brought a memory to her mind of her deceased daughter, for she wiped the tears from her eyes as quickly as they fell. Maggie stopped playing the flute.

"I'm *u-yo-a-ye-lv-di*," Maggie apologized. She still used the English word when unsure of the translation.

Little Bear surprised Maggie by reaching out to hug her. Mayhap the gesture was more for Maggie than herself. She hadn't hugged Maggie since she was given to her. The tears flowed from Maggie's eyes now, weeping for the mother she would, in all likelihood, never see again.

That evening, thoughts of escaping the village swirled through her mind. She had gained the trust of Little Bear and others in the village. Even Nanye'hi seemed to trust her more with each passing day. She would need to get to the creek. It would be more difficult to follow her trail if she stayed in the water. As fast as her mind calculated an escape plan, her memory of the afternoon with the grandson of Kanagagota made her heart flutter against her chest. Up until this exchange, all Indians had been savages to Maggie. But the kindnesses shown to her in the village softened her image of these proud and brave people. She went to sleep remembering the melody of the flute and Oukonunaka.

Maggie awoke before Degataga and Little Bear. She dressed quickly and moved toward the door, glancing back at the sleeping couple, she stuffed the flute into the pocket of her dress. She inhaled, holding her breath as she lifted the latch on the door. The wood block popped as Maggie raised the latch. She froze, sure the sound alerted Little Bear. She looked over her shoulder, neither stirred.

Satisfied she was successful in making it out the door, Maggie pulled the latch and walked away from the cabin.

For a moment, she decided to sneak off to the creek. She knew the dogs would bark if she got close to the wooden gate. It was early, and if she planned to escape, she would have to go now.

Daylight was still moments away. Maggie moved stealthily as a bobcat as she stayed behind the cabins and summer dwellings, hoping to make her escape.

She scampered down the well-worn path to the creek. It was here that Maggie carried water with Little Bear each day.

Her legs felt unsteady as she reached the creek's bank. Her heart thumped wildly in her chest as she paused to catch her breath.

She stepped into the cool water, trying not to make any splashing sounds that might give away her escape. The sun would soon make its appearance over the cedar trees to the east of the village. In a short time, the whole village would be awake. Degataga and Little Bear would find Maggie no longer asleep on her pallet.

She looked up the creek, with its curves and cane brakes. She had no idea where to run. They would find her, then what? The snap of a twig startled her, causing her to jump.

She turned, expecting to be dragged back to her Indian mother and father. Instead, she saw Oukonunaka. In his hand was a fox he'd caught in a trap.

"Ahyoka?" He approached with caution.

Maggie's knees swayed like corn stalks in the wind. It was only Oukonunaka, mayhap she could get away before the others found her. She decided to bolt running into the creek.

"*A-ga-ti-di-s-di, ga-lu-tsv ga-so-hi*!" He ran after her. Wait. Come back.

Maggie's feet sloshed in the creek, unable to out run Oukonunaka. When he caught up to her, his arm reached around her waist, pulling her out of the creek.

"Let me go!" She twisted against his chest. Her voice trailed into a whimper. "Please, I want to go home."

He didn't understand all of her words but understood what she was trying to do.

Maggie knew her chance to escape might not come again. She crumpled to the ground, pulling her knees up to her chest. The sound of her sobbing echoed through the woods.

Little Bear awoke to find Maggie already awake and gone. She searched the other cabins of the girls who befriended her, Tayanita and Galilani. Not finding her with them, she hurried to the dwelling of Awiagina.

She called out, alerting others that Ahyoka was missing. Several warriors set out to find Maggie. They followed the sound of her speaking down by the creek's edge. Maggie stood, moving closer to Oukonunaka.

Oukonunaka explained to the warriors that the two had come to check his trap, at which he displayed the dead fox by its tail. Maggie didn't understand what he said but saw their looks of anger disappear. Maggie played her part, smiling at the warriors.

Little Bear and Degataga ran all the way down to the creek. She grabbed Maggie by her arm but Degataga rebuked her. It was clear to Maggie escaping would have been futile. Oukonunaka had protected her secret, and for whatever reason she was grateful.

Maggie obediently followed Little Bear and Degataga back to the village. Gazing over her shoulder, she smiled at Oukonunaka. He hurried to catch up to her, handing her the flute.

"*Wa-do*," she said, and it was understood she meant it for more than returning her flute.

Maggie guessed it was late October. The forest turned into a cornucopia of vibrant colors. The scarlet maple, golden chestnut, and burnt orange oak leaves blanketed the mountains. Maggie was reminded of her mother's quilt covering her rope bed.

Several of the warriors joined the British in fighting the colonists. Maggie wondered if her father went off to join the Continental Army?

The crisp air signaled the ushering in of fall in the mountains. Maggie pulled her blanket around her shoulders as she walked out of their cabin. She had but a moment to be idle, as Little Bear took her by the arm to do chores that awaited her.

The women were busy tanning the hide of a large doe. The hide was staked to four sharp sticks in the ground. Two squaws rubbed small globs of the doe's brain onto the hide.

Maggie and Tayanita cut the venison into strips. Galilani, U-da-nv-ti and Ac-wi-i-na-ge-e-hi placed the strips onto the racks to dry. Preparing for the winter was essential, not knowing whether game would be plentiful in the winter months.

Maggie helped Little Bear collect the last of the gourds from the garden. The pumpkins were cut into strips and hung from thin cords above the mantle.

The tribe's supply of salt was dangerously low. The salt licks some distance from the village were a gathering place for the deer and other game that needed the essential mineral. On this day, preparations were being made for a journey back to the licks to gather as much of the mineral as they could carry.

The trip would take several days. With so many of the warriors away helping the British in the war, their village was vulnerable to attacks from the settlers as well as the Chicka-mauga Indians. The two tribes were at war, and Nanye'hi, along with a group of warriors, traveled to the Watauga River valley to seek support against the southern Indians.

Little Bear prepared to join her husband on the trek. Maggie feared her father and the other men may be going to the salt licks to load their horses with the precious preservative, too. What if the two groups visited the lick at the same time? The thought gnawed at her.

Maggie asked Little Bear if she could go. In her broken Cherokee, she sounded sincere. The thought of being close to Boonesborough emboldened her to nag her Indian mother.

"No," she replied. "You will stay with Awiagina." Maggie understood most of the words.

Degataga left the cabin without saying a word to Maggie. He was a quiet man, and Maggie hadn't heard him utter more than half a dozen words since he moved into their dwelling.

Little Bear finished packing the small pouch with strips of venison and dried pumpkin for the journey to the salt lick. Before she joined her husband, she put her arms around Maggie.

"You are a good daughter." The words were all Little Bear could utter in the way of a goodbye to Maggie. She gathered her to her bosom, the smell of smoke and buckskin filled Maggie's nostrils. She found the language easier to under-stand and was able to converse with others, when they spoke to her.

Maggie missed her mother and father's embraces. The Indian mother had been good to Maggie, despite her being a payment for the life of her deceased daughter.

The exchange was brief. Little Bear lifted the rope and wood block latch and joined Degataga and the others.

The crisp air carried the puffs of smoke from the early morning fire pits. A slight gust of wind encouraged the crimson and orange leaves to float aimlessly to the ground. Golden rays of sunlight peeked through the pine boughs, illuminating the side of the Council House. Maggie felt the warmth on her face as she waited for what would happen next.

For this journey, the group would be gone for several days. They would use a dugout canoe, made from a large birch tree. The process was quite fascinating to Maggie.

The trunks of trees would be hollowed out with hot coals. Then, the insides were scraped with sharp stones. Birch trees were used for the canoes, because they were very light, and the bark was waterproof. If there were no birch trees available, they used another type of tree, and covered it with birch bark. They needed trees that were light because sometimes, if the river ended or became harder to paddle in, they would pick up the canoe and walk until they could paddle again.

Little Bear, Degataga, Woya, Chea Sequah, and Tsiyi carried two dugout canoes from the village to the creek. They were on their way to retrieve the coveted mineral that would provide the village a preservative. Harvesting salt was a time consuming and labor-intensive job. Once harvested, it would be boiled, dried, and scraped from the boiling pot. It would keep the meat edible throughout the winter months.

Oukonunaka and the other young braves stood together. It was clear they wanted to be part of something. With so many of the warriors away in the war with the British and colonists, it left only the older men and young boys to defend the village. Several of the warriors, like Five Killer, remained to defend the village. Nanye'hi and Bryant Ward returned from visiting another tribe of Cherokee at Cowee, in North Carolina. Maggie felt a pang of uneasiness settle inside her. She looked back to see Awiagina waving to the hunting party, pausing from the task at hand.

Maggie joined the elder woman in collecting persimmons that had fallen to the ground. The two filled their baskets with the tart fruit. During the winter, they would eat dried fruits and nuts, along with whatever game they could trap and shoot.

Maggie carried the fruit back to the drying racks. Together, she and Awiagina placed the persimmons on a large rock to dry in the sun. Several of the children were given the task of swatting flies and keeping the varmints away. Pumpkin and squash were dried in the same manner.

"Come, Ahyoka. Tonight, you will stay in my wigwam." Her knees creaked as she bent to pick up her basket. She reached for Maggie to steady herself.

Maggie put her arm through the elder woman's, a feeling of warmth coursed through her body. She felt a kinship with Awiagina. The two entered the wigwam. The wooden door was pulled closed and Awiagina lit a pine knot and sat it on the dirt floor. She busied herself by the fire pit preparing a meal of pemmican, wild onion, and potatoes. The grease popped in the clay cooking pot.

Maggie tucked her legs underneath her and sat on the mat near the hearth. She tried to think of her words before speaking. Her command of the Cherokee language was simple at best.

"May I help you, Grandmother?" Maggie asked. It was obvious she wanted to please the elder woman.

Awiagina's thin lips turned upwards, exposing her gums, save for the two teeth on top and two on the bottom.

Maggie and Awiagina ate their meal together in silence. Maggie missed hearing her family chatter around their table at mealtime. She understood more Cherokee than she could speak. When they had finished their meal, Maggie took the bowls made from dried gourds and wiped them clean with a wet cloth.

She looked over her shoulder to see Awiagina's head go down and back up again. Maggie stifled a laugh. The elder woman yawned. She went to roll out a pallet for Maggie.

"I would like to sleep in my wigwam," Maggie said. She tried rephrasing the words in Cherokee. After two tries, she became frustrated.

Awiagina patted Maggie's hand. She nodded, giving Maggie permission.

A brilliant pink and purple sunset sank low behind the birch trees. Maggie walked along the row of small wigwams of wattle and daub until she came to the small cabin she shared with Little Bear and Degataga. She felt a chill raise gooseflesh on her arms. She added wood to the fire and looked at the sparse dwelling.

She'd gathered strips of birch bark and used pieces of charcoal from the fire pit to write in the makeshift diary. She soon found the underside of the bark made an excellent substitute for paper. She kept it tucked underneath her pallet. She missed her paper diary and pencil.

On this day, she took out a small section of bark and wrote a short entry:

On this date, the Indians went for salt and game. Maggie Diele.

She put the bark under her pallet and took out the flute Oukonunaka made her.

She placed her fingers on the smooth holes and brought the end to her mouth. She'd practiced each evening in front of the fire. Tonight, she tried to play a melody she'd heard her mother hum but couldn't remember the exact tune.

The flute sang like a bird when Oukonunaka played it, but her attempt sounded more like an owl in the oak tree screeching.

She listened to a conversation coming from outside her wigwam. It sounded like Oukonunaka and Ulinawi. The young braves were taking their turn guarding the village.

Maggie's eyelids fluttered as she tried to keep from falling asleep. She watched the image of the pine knot's flame dancing on the wall of the wigwam. For a fleeting moment, she entertained the thought of running away. With Little Bear on a hunting trip, she had no one watching her every move. Her first attempt had been a failure.

She sank back on the pallet.

What will become of me? What must Mama and Papa think has happened to me?

She felt hot tears slide down her tanned cheeks.

Will anyone come for me?

Maggie thought of her best friend, Mary Katherine. How she wished to have a chance to listen to her talk about the boys of Boonesborough. She thought of her doll, Elizabetha.

Mayhap Mama has her close by tonight.

Maggie heard the far-off rumbles of thunder. Gusts of wind whipped throughout the village bringing down small limbs from the chestnut and birch trees. She tried to sleep amidst the thunderclaps and bursts of bright lights dancing across the night sky.

She feared the wigwam would be blown away in the gusts of wind howling on the other side of the doorway. When the following crash of thunder brought with it a gust of wind that blew the door covering into the wigwam, Maggie screamed. She hastily pulled on her moccasins and covered her head with her coverlet of rabbit skins and ran through pouring rain to Awiagina's wigwam.

"Awiagina, please let me in," Maggie shouted over the thunder. In her panic, she spoke the words in English. Her hair dripped into her eyes as she pulled the rabbit skin cover over her head. She beat her hand against the wooden door.

"Ahyoka, come inside."

Maggie heard Oukonunaka's voice from his uncle's wigwam. She didn't understand why Awiagina didn't answer her repeated banging against the door.

"*Wado,* Oukonunaka," Maggie said, ducking into the low doorway.

He shared a dwelling with his uncle, aunt, and two sisters. The inside of the wigwam was cramped, but dry. She thanked Oukonunaka again, feeling less afraid. Once again, Oukonunaka came to her rescue.

Through her broken Cherokee, she explained the storm blew open her doorway and it frightened her. How much they understood she didn't know, but his sisters took her wet covering and gave her a dry blanket to wrap around her shoulders.

"Awiagina sleeps like the bear in the winter cave," Oukonunaka said, holding his hands over his ears and making a snoring sound. His sisters snickered at his theatrics. Maggie laughed at Oukonunaka's imitation of the elder woman.

The storm raged outside, but the dwelling of wattle and daub held tight. Maggie felt safe with her friend, even though a feeling of dread crept into her deepest thoughts.

Chapter 21

Two weeks passed from the time Little Bear and the others went to the salt licks. Little Bear's wigwam suffered considerable damage to the roof during the storm. Maggie helped Oukonunaka and his uncle, Immokalee, patch the gaps in the roof with new strips of bark and daub. Salali and Adsila, Oukonunaka's sisters, worked with Maggie and her slow understanding of their language. Each day they walked into the woods and schooled Maggie in the basic of words.

Her friends, Tayanita and Galilani spoke to Maggie in Cherokee. She was ignored if she spoke English. She found this practice annoying and rude. She often said words that were incorrect, sometimes bringing a roar of laughter from the other young adults. She conversed in broken words and gestures at first, however, she even impressed Nanye'hi with her limited command of the language when she returned from her trip to see Dragging Canoe, her cousin.

Maggie gathered the last of the nuts that had fallen. They were buried beneath the dried leaves that were now brittle and brown. She carried them, along with a string of fish Oukonunaka caught for her. She sat her goods on the large stone beside the fire pit. She knew nothing of gutting a fish, and the thought of seeing the insides of any animal made her queasy.

Awiagina took a piece of flint that she'd been using as a knife and quickly sliced open the fish. The entrails were taken out and thrown on the ground. The dogs feasted on the innards of the cleaned fish.

Once the fish were gutted, a sharp stick was shoved through the mouth and out the tail fin of the fish. It was placed over the fire to roast. Maggie prepared a bread from the cornmeal Awiagina had ground and placed it in a clay pot to bake within the hot coals.

As they waited for the meal to finish cooking, Awiagina rose from the stump she used as a stool and disappeared into the wigwam. Within a few moments, she returned with something in her wrinkled hand.

"For you, granddaughter." She held out a small pouch covered in tiny beads. The pouch was made from the softest deerskin and was attached to a cord that went around Maggie's neck. Inside, Awiagina placed sprigs of sage. Maggie put the sage to her nose, smelling its woodsy scent.

"Thank you, grandmother. It's beautiful." She made the old woman smile as she spoke the words in Cherokee.

"It will protect you, Ahyoka, from the evil spirits." She patted Maggie's hand.

Maggie was unsure what she was referring to but slipped the cord around her neck. She was proud to wear such a fine gift.

A dog barking at the palisade doors caught their attention. The dog growled and lunged at the wooden doors. Several other dogs barked as if alerting the village of impending danger.

Five Killer and Kanuna approached the door with caution, carrying rifles over their shoulders.

Maggie moved closer to Awiagina. She saw Oukonunaka and other young braves take their tomahawks and war clubs to join the others.

Maggie imagined Chickamauga warriors storming into the village, scalping and murdering the likes of them. She shuddered as fear rose inside her.

Oukonunaka turned to Maggie and his sisters who were sitting nearby, "Run to the creek, wait there."

She grabbed onto Awiagina's hand and helped her to stand. The two sisters of Oukonunaka, Maggie's friends, Tayanita and Galilani, hurried toward the river. Nanye'hi and her husband went into their wigwam and returned with their own guns.

The dogs continued barking until the chief, Kanuna, motioned for Five Killer to open the doors. The dogs sensed something was about to happen and moved out of the way. Oukonunaka held fast to his tomahawk, ready to sink the blade into a Chickamaugan's head if needed. The doors slowly opened and Tsiyi, the warrior who returned with scalps on a previous hunting trip, fell onto the ground, a crimson stain covered his chest and back.

The rest of the warriors rushed the door, searching for the rest of the party.

Nanye'hi motioned for the men to carry Tsiyi to her wigwam. Once inside, she and Woya, a medicine woman, began assessing his wounds. He appeared to have gone days without food or drink, so a gourd full of water was placed up to his mouth.

Weak from loss of blood and lack of water, he choked on the first sip from the dipper. Woya saw the hole where a musket ball passed through Tsiyi's shoulder. The women cleaned the wound, applying moss to the hole to lessen the blood flow.

Oukonunaka ran over the hill to the creek where the women and young girls waited. Maggie rose from her spot on the creek bank.

"It's Tsiyi. He's bleeding."

"Little Bear and Degatuga?" Maggie asked as they made their way back to the village.

"He came back alone. Nanye'hi and Woya are tending to him."

Maggie helped Awiagina back to her wigwam. She sat with Oukonunaka outside Nanye'hi's wigwam.

Inside, Tsiyi told of their fate. The hunting party came upon a group of colonists who were camped near the salt lick. Little Bear saw the hunters first, alerting her husband. The settlers fired from a distance and hit Little Bear with a lead ball to her head. The next shot took Degataga in the chest, knocking him back against a tree. He was dead before he slid to the ground. He and Chea Sequah were able to get a shot off before getting away from their pursuers.

As they were making their escape, Chea Sequah was hit in the back of the head with a lead ball. Tsiyi didn't realize he'd been shot until he reached the river. He crawled to a hollow tree nearby to spend the night. He wasn't sure how long he stayed, but he stayed close to the river bank until he made his way back to the village.

Maggie's eyes grew large as saucers when Nanye'hi finally emerged from her wigwam. She came over to Maggie, sitting beside her on the log bench.

"Ahyoka, your mother, Little Bear, has been killed by the whites. All of the hunting party were killed, except Tsiyi." Nanye'hi put her arm around Maggie.

Maggie understood the words Nanye'hi said. She didn't love Little Bear, but she had been a kind substitute for her own mother.

"What will become of me, Nanye'hi?" Maggie's fears returned.

"Go to Awiagina's cabin tonight, Ahyoka. You will stay with her this evening." Nanye'hi went back into the wigwam, leaving Maggie to return to the empty dwelling she shared with Little Bear and Degataga to pack her things.

Chapter 22

Maggie sat on a pallet beside the fire staring at the dancing flames. Awiagina sat on a stool working beads onto the toe of a pair of moccasins. Maggie loved the elder woman. She had tried keeping her heart closed to Little Bear, and now she was gone. Maggie's eyes pooled with tears.

"Little one, your mother is with the Great Spirit. She will walk through this village again to check on you when it is dark, and you sleep." Awiagina put her beadwork on the floor beside her.

Maggie understood the things Awiagina said to her, not fully grasping the concept of Little Bear being a spirit that wandered the earth.

She laid her head in Awiagina's lap. Her heart was sad, not only for the loss of the hunting party, but also because now she belonged to no one.

"What will become of me, Grandmother?" Maggie felt the leathery hand of Awiagina pull the hair back from her face in a rhythmic pattern.

"That is for Beloved Woman to decide, child."

The words carried the importance of Nanye'hi as the Beloved Woman and Peace Chief.

Maggie curled up on her pallet. She thought about Little Bear and the others lying in the woods without a proper burial. She remembered her little brother and how her parents grieved over the little pine box that was lowered into the dark, cold earth. Maggie felt sad Little Bear was denied a proper burial, as were the others.

She listened as Awiagina sang a low mourning song. Maggie pulled her coverlet up to her chin and closed her eyes. She listened to the sad song until she went into a deep sleep.

The clans gathered in the Council House for discussion about the deaths of Little Bear, Chea Sequah, Degataga and Woya. The War Chief addressed the massacre and the grave condition of Tsiyi.

The different clans spoke in accordance to their location around the arbor. Many argued for taking a large war party back to Kentucke to retrieve the remains for burial. Others spoke for attacking the settlements in and around the Licks. Maggie listened as the passionate speeches were given.

Little Bear left no family members to mourn her death, other than Maggie, her adopted daughter.

Nanye'hi spoke about the war between the English and colonists. There would be more and more settlers coming into the area, and peace must be sought.

Maggie listened as Nanye'hi urged the tribe not to seek retaliation for the massacre. She looked to Maggie, addressing the tribe.

"She has fulfilled the replacement to Little Bear for avenging of the death of A-tsi-lv-s-gv. Little Bear and Awinita walk the earth together in their spirit forms. I give Ahyoka to her people, or she can remain with our people. I leave that decision up to Ahyoka."

Maggie understood Nanye'hi to say she was free to return to her family. After months of thinking about escaping, her mind tried to accept freedom was now a gift.

"We must avenge the deaths of our people, Nanye'hi. The whites come over the mountains like locust. Soon they will take all our hunting grounds."

"Let it be so. To avenge the deaths of those who were taken." Nanye'hi took her place beside the other chiefs.

Maggie looked across the arbor to Oukonunaka, sitting proud with his shoulders squared and face held high. She wasn't aware of the change she had undergone since her captivity, but she was leaving behind her childish ways and becoming a young woman. She'd survived being apart from her family, a fate worse than she'd ever imagined.

Oukonunaka caught Maggie staring at him from across the Council House. For a moment, he felt his ears grow hot. Not wanting to get a sharp jab from his uncle, he turned his gaze back to the Chief.

Maggie lowered her eyes, she blushed at being caught staring like a love-sick ox.

Caught in her own daydreaming, Maggie didn't realize the Council meeting was adjourned and the different clans had exited the Council House. Awiagina waited for Maggie, both belonging to the same clan, the Long Hair clan. She walked with measured steps, staying beside Awiagina.

Maggie sat beside Awiagina and ground the last of the corn from the harvest. A squirrel sitting atop the wood pile watched for a morsel to drop to the ground. Maggie took a handful of corn from a wooden basket, laying it on the grinding stone. She moved the pestle, a stone tool with a rounded end used for crushing and grinding substances, around the pile of corn. The crushed corn soon became the consistency of coarse meal.

Awiagina repeated the same process with her pestle. "Granddaughter, you mustn't hold in what you are wanting to ask." She continued turning the stone, not raising her head.

"I heard Nanye'hi say I could leave the village. I want to see my mother and father, but I . . ."

"You want to stay with old Grandmother?" she smiled, causing her eyes to pinch shut.

"I want to take you with me." Maggie's naive comment caught Awiagina off guard.

"You are Cherokee now."

The warriors made plans to retrieve the bodies near the salt lick. Bryant Ward, Nanye'hi's white husband, would be accompanying the large group leaving the following day. Maggie went with Awiagina to speak with Nanye'hi.

"Have you made a decision, Ahyoka?"

"I want to return to my parents." Maggie raised her eyes to meet the Beloved Woman's inquisitive gaze.

"What if they are no longer at your village?" Nanye'hi asked. Her meaning was lost on Maggie.

"They will be there, I know it."

"We are moving our village to join with my uncle at Chota. Many warriors are traveling to join the English in the war against the white settlers. The white settlers will be caught between the Indians and the English. Come with us, Granddaughter," Awiagina pleaded.

With a heavy heart, Maggie made her decision. She wanted to go home.

The following morning, a band of 25 warriors, along with Nanye'hi, Bryant Ward, and Maggie, prepared to travel the five-day journey back to Kentucke. Before they left the village, Oukonunaka hurried from his uncle's wigwam to ask Nanye'hi if he could accompany Maggie back to her people. Seeing the friendship the two had developed, she agreed.

Maggie hugged Tayanita and Galilani, the girls who befriended her and taught her to speak Cherokee. Each brought something to give to Maggie.

Tayanita presented her with a beaded necklace, and Giliani gave her a pair of winter moccasins she had fashioned with red tassels.

"*Wado*," Maggie said.

Each gift was placed in the hide backpack Little Bear had made for her. She had put her flute, small basket she'd made, and the medicine pouch she'd received from Awiagina inside as well.

Next came Awiagina. She carried a cornhusk doll, outfitted with a buckskin dress. "For you, Granddaughter. To remember me."

Maggie threw her arms around Awiagina and buried her face into her soft bosom. "*Wado*, Grandmother. I love you." She hugged her until Nanye'hi told her it was time to go. She placed the pack across her back, adjusting the load she now must carry on the journey back to Boonesborough.

This time, they would not travel by water. The dogs were fastened with travois to carrying back the dead over land. As they walked out of the tall wooden doors, Maggie glanced back at the village and waved goodbye to the Indians she'd grown to love.

The warriors carried English rifles, war clubs, and tomahawks. Bryant Ward rode his chestnut mare and carried a large rifle with a powder horn across his dark blue military jacket.

The likelihood of another attack was high and having Ward along to speak to any white settlers or English military would prove advantageous. Maggie remained silent, unless spoken to. She walked beside the tall and lanky Oukonunaka.

Oukonunaka's hair was gathered at the top of his head in a knot. He'd not yet plucked away the hairs on the sides. His moccasins reached to his knees and accentuated his long legs. The long knife he carried hung at his waist inside a buckskin sheath. Across his back he carried a rifle presented to him by his uncle. The other warriors walked in single file, stepping in the footprints of the one before him.

Maggie knew the trek back to Kentucke was a somber trip, not to mention dangerous. She tried to keep her excitement contained. In a few weeks she would be sitting in her parents' cabin in Boonesborough. Her brother had celebrated a birthday since her captivity. She missed him and his teasing. How wonderful it would be to see her friend, Mary Katherine, again.

As she walked toward the mountains that separated the Cherokee lands and the Virginia county of Kentucke, she realized the two worlds in which she'd lived were as different as night and day.

Maggie imagined it was into the month of November. The trees were already losing their leaves and the squirrels fought for every nut on the ground. The forest floor was covered now with the leaves that had swirled down from the tall trees in the forest.

On this day, the sky was the bluest of blues with the absence of clouds. Walking through the dense forest obscured the view of the glorious sky. The sunbeams reached through the canopy of dried leaves on the branches and shone on the forest floor--first in one area, then another.

Maggie marveled at their silent passage through the forest, even though there were twenty-five warriors, Nanye'hi, Bryant Ward, and herself. Maggie listened to the sounds of the forest as they continued walking in silence.

A hawk soared in the sky and seemed to follow them each day. The warriors took turns keeping watch while the others slept. They moved at a fast pace and took little time to rest during the day. They ate pemmican, venison jerky, and persimmons. When they were able to stop for a moment to rest or relieve themselves, Maggie and Oukonunaka spoke.

"I have asked Beloved Woman if I might walk you to your village."

"I don't know where we are." Maggie didn't remember coming through this area with Five Killer.

"We are close to the place where Little Bear, Woya, Degataga, and Chea Sequah were killed," Oukonunaka answered.

Five Killer motioned for the others to follow him. He knew this path well, having traveled it several times over the past few months. He had brought Maggie on this same trail four months earlier. The journey to the salt licks took over two weeks to reach. It would be another week to Boonesborough.

Maggie conversed in a mix of Cherokee and English. She was quick to pick up the language but found herself moving back and forth when speaking with others. The Cherokee were able to converse in English, having been exposed to the English traders and with missionaries coming in contact with the various Cherokee villages.

Maggie kept her fear of being left in the forest to herself. On the morning of the fifteenth day, the entourage reached the salt licks. The gruesome sight of the attack brought a wave of nausea over Maggie. She turned her head away from Little Bear's decomposing corpse. The others were still lying where they fell. It was evident wild animals had found the bodies and carried off parts of each.

The dogs barked, aware of a strong scent of death. Nanye'hi carried the blankets to where the bodies lay. The warriors didn't bother burying the white settlers who were killed in the massacre.

Maggie made herself look at the faces of the white men. She felt the venison jerky churning in her stomach and abruptly and violently leaving her body. She fell to her knees, unable to stop retching until the contents of her stomach were gone.

"Ahyoka, are these men from your village?" Nanye'hi inquired, seeing Maggie's reaction.

"No. I don't recognize them." Maggie felt weak and afraid she was on the verge of vomiting again.

"Five Killer and I will take you as far as the river, then you must walk the rest of the way back to your village alone," Nanye'hi stated.

"I will walk with Ahyoka," Oukonunaka offered. He wanted to spend more time with Maggie before she went back to live among the whites.

"Very well, Oukonunaka." Nanye'hi watched as the warriors wrapped what was left of the bodies in blankets and placed them on the travois. On the remaining travois, pots filled with the salt were loaded to be hauled over the mountains to their village called Coyatee.

It was here the warriors divided their numbers. They would retaliate for the deaths of their people, but Boonesborough would not be attacked during this raid.

The remaining warriors traveled south with the travois carrying the deceased and baskets filled with saltpeter. Maggie, Five Killer, Bryant Ward, and Oukonunaka traveled with Maggie to the north.

The somber travelers made their way out of the cane brakes and walked through dark and foreboding forests. Maggie's heart raced as she thought of her family seeing her again after thinking she had been killed by the savages.

Maggie watched Nanye'hi, her long black hair gathered in a braid at the back of her neck. Her dark eyes weren't cold or murderous as others had called the Indian's eyes. She had seen kindness and compassion in them. She carried a walking stick carved from one of the mighty oak trees that fell during a recent storm. The terrain was steep and slick because of the fallen leaves, treacherous to those in moccasined feet.

Twice Maggie slipped but Oukonunaka caught her before she hit the ground. Five Killer had brought Maggie through the same path, only her tight shoes caused her feet to blister and bleed. She remembered he'd allowed her to ride atop the horse he rode back from his trip to the Ohio River.

At dusk, they stopped for the night. The temperature fell sharply during the evening, and frost covered the leaves and pine trees in the forest. Maggie pulled close Degataga's buffalo robe. She'd rescued it before his and Little Bear's possessions were burned. She was thankful for the kindness shown to her.

Five Killer and Bryant Ward took turns watching for wolves and bear in the area while Nanye'hi, Maggie, and Oukonunaka dozed against an ancient elm tree. They huddled together to keep warm as the fire burned low. An owl kept watch above, 'hoo hooting' while Five Killer kept a keen eye on the forest.

When Maggie was able to doze, she dreamed of her mother and the smell of rose water perfume that she'd worn when they lived in Culpeper. She saw herself carrying her wooden doll, Elizabetha, to the apple orchard in their lower field. There she sat under an apple tree, enjoying the warm summer breeze.

A scream came from across the orchard where her mother was picking juicy apples. Maggie watched as an Indian grabbed her mother by the hair and quickly lifted her scalp with one fell swoop. The nightmarish scene jolted Maggie from her slumber. Even with the frost on her robe, she felt the sweat on her forehead. Embarrassed, she tried calming herself as the others slept around her.

Bryant Ward took his turn at watch while Five Killer pushed himself against a fallen log, holding his rifle close. In another hour it would be time to start moving again.

The travelers walked over cold, wet ground. A heavy rain the previous day left the ground muddy and marshy. Nanye'hi and Maggie gathered moss for such an occasion while stopping two nights prior. Seeing the need to keep their feet dry, they lined the insides of their moccasins with the warm moss. At one point, Bryant lifted Nanye'hi up to ride on the back of his horse.

Maggie and Oukonunaka walked together, neither wanting to break the silence. Maggie knew they were getting closer to the river. They had seen buffalo and deer following the trace since leaving the salt licks. With each step, Maggie's heart beat faster, the excitement of seeing her mother and father giving her a shot of adrenaline to keep walking, even though her legs and feet ached.

Bryant turned to tell Maggie they would be at the river's edge soon, the very spot she and Five Killer crossed some four months earlier. He hopped down from his horse and led the stallion down the side of the rocky terrain. The temperature turned colder, and breath was visible from both man and beast. Maggie pulled the buffalo robe tighter around her. The wind caused her eyes to water. She longed for her pair of woolen gloves back in the cabin.

By the time the sun stood above them, the river was in sight. They trudged down a steep embankment to the cane brakes, walking single file and guarding each step. When they reached the river's edge, a light snow began falling. It was here that Nanye'hi bid farewell to Maggie.

Five Killer gave her some of the jerky in his pouch around his chest. They would be three weeks from the village.

"Keep walking with the sun to your left."

Maggie tried to swallow, but her throat felt like a ball of wool. It hadn't sunk in until this very moment that she would be alone for the rest of the journey. She stood at the bank of the river, looking at the rushing water. It was only up to her ankles, but the current moved swift and strong. Nanye'hi embraced Maggie for a moment and released her. Maggie put one foot into the cold water, feeling the chill rise from her feet to her head, feeling a pinch of pain as she started to cross the river.

"Ahyoka, wait!" Oukonunaka entered the water.

"Oukonunaka, you must come with us," Bryant called to the young warrior.

"I won't leave Ahyoka until she is back with her village," he said defiantly.

Maggie grasped his outstretched hand. Together, the two set out to cross the river. The water rushed over Maggie's feet and rose to her calves. Her buckskin dress soaked in the water that rushed underneath her. She made sure her pack was lifted high on her back.

Oukonunaka turned to see Bryant and Nanye'hi watching from the embankment. He led Maggie across the river to the other side, careful to not fall on the slippery stones. Once Maggie was safely across, Nanye'hi and Bryant raised an arm. They led their horse up and over the steep embankment and finally out of site.

Oukonunaka and Maggie moved quickly through the tall grass and cane growing thick along the river. Maggie knew it was best to keep hidden. She feared for Oukonunaka's safety.

As they walked along the river, above them two hawks circled. The pair had followed the group since they left the Indian village.

Maggie was exhausted from three weeks of walking, but she kept up with Oukonunaka. She periodically stopped to adjust her pack on her back. The scenery was familiar, and she recognized the bluff on the opposite side of the river. This was the spot she was taken by Five Killer.

"You can turn back now, I will go the rest of the way alone." Maggie grabbed Oukonunaka's wrist, pulling him back.

Oukonunaka looked toward the village ahead. He wanted to walk Maggie into the village and see her reunited with her mother and father.

"I will go, but I will always remember you Ahyoka." He put his fist to his heart. Around his neck, he wore a necklace with a bear claw hanging from the leather braid. He took it from his neck. "For you to remember me."

"*Wado*. I'll never forget you." Her propriety lost, she leaned into Oukonunaka and kissed his cheek.

She hadn't thought of kissing a boy before, but Maggie felt like she was no longer a little girl. Oukonunaka was taken by surprise. Maggie turned and walked toward Boonesborough. Amidst the joy of seeing her family again was a sadness of knowing she would never see her friend again.

Chapter 23

Maggie followed the path to the lower fields near the river. She saw the cows drinking from the river, and two boys stood with walking sticks to herd them back to the corral. Maggie's eyes strained to see who the boys were. She didn't recognize either of them. As she came within view, the boys took off running to the village palisade. Maggie ran to the spot where the boys were standing. She heard them yelling, "Indians!"

Before she could take in the fact that she was back in Boonesborough, she was being surrounded by men with guns. She spoke her name, but it was drowned out by the commotion.

Maggie looked every bit the Indian. Her face was tan from months in the sun without a bonnet to shield her skin. Her buckskin dress and deerskin boots resembled that of the Indian women who came to trade at Martin's Station. The buffalo robe she wore around her shoulders swallowed her small frame.

Maggie's shoulder length hair, once dark brown, now lightened to show sun-streaked strands of gold woven into the long braid. She found the voices loud and confusing, talking to her all at the same time.

"What is your name?" Flanders Callaway asked.

"Maggie, Maggie Diele," she said, her voice squeaked.

"Are you alone? Are there more redskins with you?" He dragged her away from the river and through the onlookers.

"I'm alone. I was taken by the Cherokee when Jemima Boone, Fanny, and Betsy Callaway were taken from the river."

The men stared in disbelief. She spoke the truth about the Callaway sisters and Jemima Boone, but she didn't resemble the young Diele girl in her Indian regalia.

By the time they hustled Maggie through the tall wooden doors entering Fort Boonesborough, a crowd had gathered upon hearing word of an Indian in the fort.

Rebecca and Daniel Boone came from their cabin hearing the commotion. Maggie saw Rebecca and broke from Flanders' grasp.

"Mrs. Boone, where are my mama and papa? I'm Maggie Diele," she said, finding her voice.

Rebecca took her hands, lifting Maggie's face, days of being without a pitcher of water evident.

She studied Maggie's face, then pulled her to her breast. "Praise Jesus! This is the Diele girl, but how?"

"Child, how did you escape your Cherokee captors alive?" Daniel asked.

"Where are my parents and brother, Will?" Maggie looked all around, searching the faces in the crowd. "My friend, Mary Katherine? She was with me that day."

"Were you harmed, child?" Rebecca put her at arm's length, studying her Indian attire.

"No, ma'am. They treated me kindly. But please, take me to my mama and papa." Maggie felt her eyes pool with tears.

"Maggie, your parents, along with the McCampbell's and Grundy's, left last month." Rebecca's words cut Maggie to the quick.

"What? . . . Why? Didn't they search for me?" Maggie started to sob, no longer able to contain her emotions.

"Child, they searched. But they came to believe you were . . ." Rebecca stopped short of saying what Maggie feared.

"They left?" Maggie felt her knees give way.

Daniel carried Maggie into their cabin. She came to as he lowered her onto the bed.

"Daniel, leave us. She needs her rest." Rebecca smiled at Maggie, "and time for woman talk."

Maggie quickly rose from the bed, not wanting to damage the contents of her backpack. Rebecca reached for Maggie's hand.

"Let's get you out of those clothes and clean you up. A good brushing and scrubbing are in order."

Maggie pulled away, wanting no part in the invitation. "I'm fine. No, thank you."

"Maggie, did the Indians hurt you?" Rebecca's question took Maggie a moment to understand.

"No! They were kind to me, always." Maggie was indignant and squared her shoulders.

"Well, that's for sure something to be thankful. Your parents and several others left the beginning of October. Said they were going back to Virginia. The Indians attacked in late August. Several men and two of our women-folk were killed. After that, several families packed up and left."

The words were like hot coals on her heart. How could they leave without knowing?

"Your parents grieved you, darlin'." Rebecca put her arm around Maggie, feeling her tense.

"Thank you for telling me," Maggie said without emotion.

"Are you hungry, child?" Rebecca stirred the stew she prepared for the Boone's supper. "Our brood seems to always be hungry." Her laughter filled the cabin.

"Yes, ma'am. Thank you." Maggie kept her pack on her back, sitting on the edge of the stool Rebecca provided at the table. She ate a bowl of the greasy stew. She had gotten used to a different diet while in captivity. The stew filled her stomach and sent a warm and satisfied feeling throughout her body.

"Maggie, we are crowded in the cabin with all our young'ins, but the McCampbell's cabin at the end of the fort is empty. If you'd like, I'll fix you a bed for tonight. Tomorrow we will get you with a family to tend you."

"I am grateful for your kindness, Mrs. Boone. Thank you." Maggie finished the last of the stew. She filled her cup for a second helping of apple cider.

After she finished eating, Rebecca tried keeping inquisitive residents of the fort from bombarding her with questions. She was thankful everyone kept their distance, with a promise she would tell of her captivity on the morrow.

The cabin wasn't as she remembered when Mary Katherine and her family lived there. Even though it had only been unoccupied a few weeks, the spiders had laid claim to the place. Maggie shuddered.

The Boone's built a fire in the cabin, and Levina Boone and her youngest sister made a pallet for Maggie. She felt their eyes on her as she watched them busy readying the cabin. Their compassionate smiles made Maggie feel she would let out a war whoop. The sorry looks were more than she could bear.

After they left, she tried to make sense of her predicament. If she had stayed with Awiagina, at least she would have someone who loved her. She opened her backpack, looking at the gifts she'd received.

"Dear Lord, tell me what to do. I'm alone . . ."

As she watched the flames flicker up the chimney, Maggie was distracted by a sound outside the cabin.

She listened through the door, it was an owl. It *hoohooted* several times. Maggie remembered hearing this same call while living with the Cherokee. It was a decoy, not a real owl.

She gathered her things. She looked about the cabin and gathered what she could to take with her. She shoved the pine knots into her pouch and tied the large blanket around her shoulders. A lone pine knot burned in a pewter candle holder, illuminating the room. She knew there would be a watchman or two keeping an eye on the fort. She'd made her decision. She had to go back to the Cherokee, if they would accept her.

Maggie remembered the wooden posts at the far corner of the fort were lower than the ones in the front. She planned to climb onto the pile of wood and go up and over the posts. She hurried past the dark cabins, careful to avoid the watchful eyes of the fort's sentries.

She saw two boys atop the newly built blockhouse, asleep at their post. She heard the owl hooting. If she planned to get out of the fort, she would go through the gate. The owl called to her and beckoned her to open the gate. No one would see her.

She reached the gate, looking one last time over her shoulder. One of the boys stirred. He looked down onto the open field beyond the fort, then back to the row of cabins below. Maggie made herself as small as she could. She hunkered down beside the blockhouse.

She waited for what seemed an eternity. Feeling bold, she scurried across the way to the double wooden doors. In one quick motion, she lifted the latch. Not stopping to shut the gate, she ran for the woods, holding tight to her buffalo robe and pack.

She felt her way into the cane brake and stopped for a moment to catch her breath. She would have to hurry to reach the river before they noticed her missing.

She heard the owl again. This time, it moved closer. She pulled tight the buffalo robe around her shoulders, feeling the cold for the first time. The adrenaline of the escape had kept her warm.

Through the woods and into the cane break came the sound of movement. Could a bear have picked up her scent? She couldn't see through the cane, it's stalks taller than she and close together. Her heart pounded against her chest as the sound of something coming towards her inched closer.

"Ahyoka? Is that you?" Oukonunaka whispered. His warm breath touched the back of her head.

"I thought . . . you left," Maggie spluttered. The tears fell in torrents from her eyes.

"I couldn't leave you, Ahyoka. Why did you run from your white mother and father?" His question brought more tears from Maggie.

"They left because they thought I was dead. Now, I have no one." Maggie's heart was broken.

"You are Cherokee. You will return to our village."

Chapter 24

Maggie held Oukonunaka's hand as they moved swift and silent through the canebrake. As daylight approached, they were crossing the river. Maggie shivered as the cold water lapped against her bare legs. Her boots were soaked. They stopped for a moment to shove moss and leaves into the soles of their boots.

"When they find I've left, they will come after me. I don't want to go with them." Maggie's eyes pleaded with Oukonunaka.

"We must hurry."

They ran as if their lives depended upon it, jumping over fallen logs, dodging low hanging tree branches. Knowing that most hunters and warriors would travel the buffalo trace near the river, Oukonunaka chose the route away from the river. This would be the route Nanye'hi and the warriors took with the dead and travois of saltpeter.

They traveled for hours before stopping to rest. With nothing but venison jerky to eat, they divided the two portions into fourths, trying to make the meager meal last longer.

Oukonunaka led Maggie through the dense forest. Darkness made travel difficult. He found a hollow tree, and this would be where they spent the night. If they only rested a couple of hours, the warriors and Nanye'hi should be a short distance away.

The hollow tree required Maggie and Oukonunaka to sit as close as two hairs on a hound's tail. Maggie didn't mind being close to Oukonunaka. She dozed off for a few moments and was back in Culpeper, sitting on the stone gate post watching her father gather pumpkins from the garden. He stopped to wave at her, lifting his tricorn cap from his head. As he went back to his work, Maggie jerked, waking from her slumber.

"We will leave as soon as it is light."

"Thank you again for staying." Maggie nestled next to Oukonunaka and closed her eyes.

The pair followed the tracks left by the heavy load on the travois. They followed the tracks for the next two days. A hawk flew overhead during the day. At night, an owl roosted in the tree above the place where they stopped for the night.

Having finished the venison jerky the day before, Maggie and Oukonunaka foraged for nuts along the way. While drinking from a spring, Oukonunaka heard men talking. He looked in every direction, putting his hands up to his mouth to take a drink. Maggie heard the voices and felt the hair on her neck tingle.

They hurried from the spring, walking single file through the dense forest. They climbed up the rocky terrain for what seemed hours. With little nutrition, both needed to stop frequently to rest.

By nightfall, they reached the summit of the mountain. Trying to avoid the hunters, they had gone off the Warrior's Path. Oukonunaka knew the village had to be nearby, but he had to admit, he was confused.

He knew to keep going in the direction they were heading. He didn't want Maggie to know they were lost.

Both were beginning to feel the effects of only having a few nuts and venison jerky for three days. Oukonunaka hadn't fired his gun for fear it would alert other Indians or settlers in their location. With the English and settlers at war, neither side would look favorably on two Indians away from their village.

"Tomorrow, we will be at our village. I lost my way when I left the Warrior's Path." He felt defeated.

"I wouldn't have made it out of the canebrake. I will always be grateful to you." Maggie smiled for the first time in days.

Maggie sat with her knees pulled up to her chest, her robe wrapped tightly around her. She watched Oukonunaka as he built a fire. They had to keep warm, even if it meant someone might see their fire.

Maggie heard the sound before he did, which was unusual. The owl hooted, alerting Oukonunaka.

The firelight cast ghoulish shadows against the trees nearby. Maggie cast a worried glance in his direction, her eyes darting from tree to tree expecting to see someone. Her scream carried through the stillness of the night when a wolf came out of the woods toward the fire. Oukonunaka loaded the rifle, keeping his eye on the wolf. In the darkness, more wolves advanced toward the fire.

"Ahyoka, stay very still."

He pulled the trigger, hitting the wolf square in the heart. The wolf dropped to the ground, but another advanced into the light of the fire.

Maggie sat paralyzed with fear. She watched Oukonunaka pull the trigger again, hitting the wolf in the side, wounding the animal. He ran off into the darkness, yelping in pain.

"I only have three bullets. We need a bigger fire." He loaded another bullet in the rifle.

Maggie dragged a large limb to the fire. Putting her foot on one end of the limb, she pulled back with all her might. The limb broke into two parts. When she placed the large limb on the fire, the flames shot up into the night sky. Embers swirled into the night air. The owl hooted from its perch above them.

Maggie and Oukonunaka huddled near the fire, listening for any sounds in the darkness. Feeling confident the other wolf was mortally wounded, the pair breathed a sigh of relief. Another limb was placed on the fire to keep them warm. Neither slept for fear of the fire going out.

The following morning, Oukonunaka spied the group of warriors who came with them carrying a small doe across the back of the first warrior.

Oukonunaka waved his rifle in the air. They halted, seeing it was Oukonunaka.

"Where is Nanye'hi?" Adahy asked.

"She and the others traveled back 8 days ago. I am bringing Ahyoka back to our village."

Seeing the two looked hungry, Adahy offered the two what pemmican was in his pack, seeing they would have venison to eat.

"Thank you. Are you going back to the village?" he asked.

"We are going to trade the skins in our canoe with white traders on the Holston. Follow the river. You will see the signs, your uncle taught you."

Maggie didn't speak but felt Oukonunaka was unsure where to go.

They followed the warriors as far as the buffalo trace on the Warrior Path. Here they stopped for the night. Adahy and the other warriors took their turns staying awake to watch for bear and bobcats which traveled the same path. Maggie listened to the sounds of the night. Hearing the owl in the tree above them, she finally closed her eyes and slept.

At sunrise, the pair put out the fire and made their way down the buffalo trace. The warriors had left while they slept.

They found a persimmon tree loaded with fruit, its bounty covered the ground. Maggie picked up several, putting them in her pack for later. They followed the river for several miles until Oukonunaka announced the village was still days away. He recognized the place where he often hunted with his uncle. They stopped to rest, and Oukonunaka caught a small fish with his blow gun as it swam near the shore. He made a fire and roasted the fish in good time. Maggie was thankful Oukonunaka had the skills to hunt and fish. She felt useless.

After they filled the small water pouch Oukonunaka carried across his chest with cold water, they continued walking along the river. The path to the village crossed through dark forests. Maggie walked behind Oukonunaka, trying to move as quietly as he through the tangle of vines and sticks. Twice she caught her arm on a thorn bush, trying not to cry out for fear her voice would travel through the forest. The pair walked for hours, only stopping to eat what little nuts and persimmons they had left.

Each morning of their journey, Oukonunaka went off to pray. Each time he returned, he looked along the river's edge. On the morning of the twelfth day, he returned from his prayers carrying a small canoe.

"Where did you find that?" Maggie exclaimed.

"A white settler met with an Indian's arrow many months ago. He is bones now. Great Spirit answered my prayer."

He motioned for Maggie to follow him back to the river's edge. Maggie saw the unfortunate trader lying on the bank of the river. Beside him lay the paddles. Oukonunaka motioned for her to pick up the paddles and follow him.

Ripples traveled over the large boulders protruding from the river. It was here the two carried the canoe across the river to the other side. They would walk along the river until it became deep enough for the canoe to travel without scraping against the rocks.

Each day, Oukonunaka used his blow gun to kill fish and small game. He skinned them and roasted the meat over the fire. Each morning, Oukonunaka thanked the Great Spirit for the animals and fish, and he thanked the fish for swimming slow, so he could catch them. Each evening, the large owl nested above them.

They had traveled on foot and canoe over two hundred miles. Tired and hungry, they reached the village after twenty-five days.

The warriors had returned the previous week, having followed the same path as Nanye'hi and Bryant Ward. A solemn burial for the fallen had already taken place. Oukonunaka's uncle and sisters feared he had been killed or captured on his way back to the village. When they saw him coming through the large gate, whoops and cries of joy filled the village.

When he appeared with Ahyoka, the girls showered them with hugs and kisses. The reunion was sweet, however, there was one Maggie longed to be reunited. She walked to Awiagina's wigwam. She called out to her, waiting for the elder woman to come to the door. When she saw Maggie, she thought she was seeing a ghost. The Cherokee believed in the spirit world, and Awiagina believed Maggie to be a ghost.

"Granddaughter, I thought you were gone from us." She started to weep.

"I've come back to stay, Grandmother. I'm all alone, my parents were not at the fort. You were right."

Awiagina took Maggie into her wigwam. She fixed a meal for her, listening to her story from beginning to end. Maggie laid her head in Awiagina's lap and cried. She was dead to her family, and from that moment on she became Ahyoka. The Cherokee were now her family.

Chapter 25

aggie started the day with new clothes. Awiagina took her other clothes to be washed at the river. Her two friends, Tayanita and Galilani, brought her a long skirt and shirt to wear. She found conversing with them easier, and she wanted to be part of the conversations around her. They delighted in braiding her hair and adorning her with woven leather sinew bracelets.

The first weeks of being back with the Cherokee were happy times for Ahyoka. She found her life with the tribe different than living with her white family. She was adopted into the tribe, they chose to have her as one of them. Even though she could take part in all of the festivals and rituals of the tribe, she missed one of her most favorite times with her white family. She missed having books and her journal to write her thoughts.

Her father's Bible had been the first book she remembered reading, and the time at night when her father read Scripture was something she longed to hear again. She used the birch bark strips cut and fashioned like a book to write in English her thoughts, much like a diary. She took strings made of animal sinew, and after punching a hole into the birch bark, tied the strings to hold the bark together like pages in a book.

Each evening, before Awiagina blew out the pine knot candle, if she stayed awake, she recorded the day's happenings. Her writings often included Oukonunaka.

December brought heavy snow. The winter of 1776 was bitter cold, and not only for the Cherokee. The Continental Army changed the course of the Revolutionary War when on December 26th, General George Washington, after crossing the Delaware River, surprised the British at Trenton and easily won the battle.

Bryant Ward returned with word of the fighting. The colonial army needed soldiers, and so did the British. The British came to different tribes asking for help in fighting the colonists. Nanye'hi spoke at the Council House about joining with the settlers, rather than the British. She preferred friendly relations rather than war.

The War Chief disagreed. The British were more inclined to leave the Indians alone, let them keep the lands they used for hunting. The settlers would be coming in waves to settle and disturb the ancient hunting grounds.

"Do we not remember Chief Dragging Canoe, your cousin, who attacked the whites and wanted our people to join with the British? What did we gain for his retaliation? Your kindness to the white settlers, bringing cattle and supplies to the whites? Our villages were burned, and our warriors joined with the British." The War Chief squared his shoulders.

"I believe we have more to gain by our alliance with the settlers. We owe many thanks to Lydia Bean, our captive, who taught us to weave and spin. She has taught us to make butter and have the milk of the cow to drink. Not all the whites want to take . . . some are willing to give."

Nanye'hi spared the life of Lydia Bean, captured prisoner, and the wife of William Bean, friend of Daniel Boone. Mrs. Bean was about to be burned at the stake by the Cherokee when Nanye'hi stamped out the embers and pulled Lydia Bean to safety. She took her into her home and nursed her back to health.

In return, Mrs. Bean shared her knowledge of dairy farming and making clothes from sheep's wool. Soon after Maggie's abduction, Lydia Bean was released to go back to her family. Nanye'hi was the first Indian to raise cattle, having the first small herd in the area.

The Council met to decide how many of the warriors would join with the British. The village of Chota, the capital of the Overland Cherokee, would be split in their decision. Nanye'hi gave her vote to the support of the settlers.

Maggie listened to the debate, curious to what would become of the people living in the Watauga Settlement where Mrs. Bean was taken. Did her parents arrive at the settlement after the Cherokee attack? Maggie could only speculate where Jacob, Christena, and Wilhelm Diele settled.

Word of the battles between the British and colonists came infrequently to Coyatee. Maggie worried Oukonunaka and the other young warriors would leave the village to take up arms with the British. She never spoke about her father being in the militia back in Culpeper. She imagined he would join with the Continental's, if needed.

The village was located near the Holston River. Maggie compared the village to Williamsburg. The Council House could seat 200, and the village had a population of nearly 200 at the time Maggie came to live with them. The cabins numbered near sixty. The Cherokee lived with the knowledge that to the British, their lives were only worth the land they occupied. They visited the village periodically, bringing trade items in exchange for the furs the village provided.

Maggie saw Bryant Ward come and go for long periods. She learned from Awiagina he was married to a white woman to the south, in South Carolina, and had children with her. After Maggie's return to the village, she learned Nanye'hi had a daughter, Elizabeth "Betsy" Ward, who lived with her white husband, Joseph Martin, in Virginia. Maggie remembered his name from their journey to Boonesborough. Her family stopped at Mr. Martin's blockhouse. They met his white wife, his bride. She had no idea he was married to Nanye'hi's daughter.

Maggie's return to Coyatee in November of 1776 marked her beginning of life as a Cherokee. She was adopted into Little Bear's clan, the Long Hair clan. Awiagina also belonged to the Long Hair clan.

In the months that followed her joining the clan, Maggie taught Awiagina to spin the wool from the sheep, something she had been taught by her mother. The two shared deep discussions as they worked together, whether it was making birch baskets or butter.

Maggie admired the elder woman. Her aged eyes twinkled as she listened to Maggie speak the Cherokee language with ease. She no longer spoke half-English, half-Cherokee.

"Grandmother, I am going to be fourteen on the ninth of May. It is almost my birthday. I remember my last birthday and the dog I received for a present."

"Dogs are much trouble, barking and wanting to eat everything."

"Yes, they bark, but I love them." Maggie continued churning the butter.

"Have you set your eyes on a certain dog?"

"Oukonunaka's hound had pups last month. There is one that I'm fond of."

A smiled washed over Awiagina's face. "Is it the dog or the warrior you are fond of?"

Maggie blushed. She tried to keep her feelings to herself where Oukonunaka was concerned, but she wasn't successful in fooling the old woman.

"Do you think Oukonunaka is fond of me?"

"He is a young brave with eyes for the pretty faces. He looks pleased when he stares at yours." She glanced at Maggie, then back to her spinning.

"He saved me from my plight after returning to Boonesborough. He brought me safely home." Maggie justified her feelings for him.

"There will be many days before I will speak to his aunt," her grandmother stated.

Maggie was learning the customs of the Cherokee. Her friend, Tayanita, was promised to Mohe. Both were sixteen years old. Maggie wondered what her future held. She imagined Oukonunaka was admired by several of the young squaws. At sixteen, he thought more of fishing and hunting than being promised to a squaw.

"You may pick out a dog, but you will take care of it." Awiagina showed no emotion.

"Oh, thank you, Grandmother!" Maggie crossed the room to hug the elder woman.

"Thank me when you are muzzling the dog for eating more than you."

On the date that she guessed was the sixth of May, Maggie awoke with an excitement she hadn't felt for months. The long winter gave way to a warm spring. On this special day, Maggie hurried into her skirt, blouse, and moccasins. She ate her breakfast in large bites, drawing a look of reprimand from Awiagina.

When she'd finished cleaning her bowl, Maggie took a brisk walk across the village to Oukonunaka's wigwam. There she found his sisters and their aunt mixing a bowl of pemmican. The wigwam was filled with pallets for sleeping, not yet rolled away.

"Hello, Ahyoka. Are you looking for Oukonunaka?" his aunt, Ayita, questioned.

"Hello. I wanted to speak with him about his dog's pups." She looked over Ayita's head but didn't see Oukonunaka.

"He goes off by himself to speak with the Spirit before he eats."

"Thank you. I will speak with him later."

The sunshine warmed her cheeks as she picked up the kindling for the fire pit in Awiagina's wigwam. The village of Coyatee bustled with activity. Maggie no longer felt the inquisitive eyes on her whenever she walked about the village. She looked as if she belonged, her skin now tanned from going without her cap and hat. She wore her hair in the traditional braid, and she preferred the doeskin dress and leggings during the winter, but now chose to wear the long skirt and blouse the squaws adopted from their English trader's fashions. With the looms and wheels, the Cherokee women fashioned their clothing from what Lydia Bean had taught them.

Maggie's birthday was less than two days away. When Bryant Ward left for his home in South Carolina, Maggie asked him what the date was, and from that day forward, kept a calendar of sorts on a strip of birch bark.

The date was May 7th. She had become a young woman while in captivity. Now she was looked upon as a young squaw, not yet of marrying age, even though families were keen on marriage arrangements for their adolescent children.

Maggie placed the kindling into the fire pit. She noticed Awiagina seemed to be feeling spry on this warm spring morning.

Outside beside the wigwam, Maggie heard a mockingbird calling roll for all the birds in the poplar tree. She remembered a time in Culpeper before her family sold their farm. Every morning, a male mockingbird flew to the elm tree outside her window.

"Ahyoka, did you choose a pup from Utina's litter?"

"Not yet, Grandmother. I will today." Maggie stirred the coals in the fire.

"Grandmother, were you married when you were younger?" Maggie's innocence brought a chuckle from Awiagina.

"Oh, yes, child." Awiagina leaned back in her chair, remembering a time long ago. "My man was tall as a pine tree, and his face was pleasant. We married when I was a year older than you are now." She gazed past Maggie, seeing a memory from a day long past.

"What was his name?"

"Cheveyo. His name means 'warrior'. He was a mighty warrior, too." The light left her eyes. "All the warriors went to battle against the Creek. "I was carrying my first child, and he promised to return to me." She brought a red cloth up to her eyes, dabbing away the tears.

"I'm sorry, Grandmother. You must have loved him very much," Maggie said softly. "What was the baby?"

"A boy child. He came soon after I learned of Cheveyo's death on the battlefield. The ghost of his father came that night and took him away from me. I named him Chaska."

Maggie felt she caused Awiagina pain in telling her story. For this, she went to her Grandmother and put her arms around her.

"I'm sorry to make you sad, Grandmother."

"No, child, it is good to remember those we love."

Maggie thought of her family. They thought she was dead. She wondered if they thought of her.

"You ask me of my husband. Are you thinking of finding a husband, Ahyoka?"

Maggie laughed, sure Awiagina was having fun with her. She let the comment pass.

It didn't matter, Awiagina knew better. Ahyoka was already setting her sights for Oukonunaka.

Two days later, Awiagina prepared a special meal for Maggie's birthday. As the two enjoyed the meal, Oukonunaka tapped on the wigwam's door. He brought a puppy from his dog's litter as his gift. Maggie's eyes beamed as the coffee colored pup licked her cheeks.

"Oh, he is perfect. Thank you!" Maggie squealed with delight. "He reminds me of the pup I had at Boonesborough. I'll call him Tracker."

Awiagina kept her feelings to herself, knowing the pup would be another mouth to feed. She reached over to scratch the pup's ear.

Chapter 26

aggie joined the other young women in the garden. Tayanita and Galilani were already hoeing a row of Three Sisters that were growing together. Corn, beans, and squash were the plants all Indians ate in their diets. The seeds of the squash or pumpkin were planted as a ground cover, their vines spreading out below the stalks of corn. The vines of the bean wound their way up the corn stalks, making the cornstalks like a bean pole.

The mood was light as the squaw did their work; it was almost time for the Green Corn Festival. There was much work to be done.

Prior to the Green Corn Festival was the ceremony held when the first green corn shoots appeared. For the festival, chanting shamans and warriors circled a cooking fire, carrying corn stalks. These first ears were boiled, removed from the pot, and tied to four tepee-like poles above the fire, as a sacred offering to the Great Spirit. The first ashes were buried, then a large new fire was kindled, to cook corn for the entire village to share in the upcoming feast and dance.

No one was allowed to eat corn, even from his own field, until the proper authority was given. When the corn was ready to be eaten, the one who had the authority announced the date for the Corn Feast and Dance.

On this occasion, great numbers of roasting ears were prepared, and all ate as freely as they desired. After this feast, everyone could have what they wished from that particular field.

During the festival, members of the tribe gave thanks for the corn, rain, sun, and a good harvest. The thanksgiving was sacred to the Indians. Folk tales were popular in the telling of what happened when thanks was not given. Some tribes even believed that they were made from corn by the Great Spirit.

The Green Corn Ceremony was traditionally celebrated during late June or early July for four days. The dates scheduled for the celebration was dependent upon the first ripened corn. The ceremony was held in the middle of the ceremonial grounds. It included the stomp dance, feather dance, and buffalo dance rituals. During the ceremonies, the people fasted, played stickball, had corn sacrificing, and took medicine. After the ceremonial fasting, they would feast. Another ritual observed was rinsing themselves in water and having prayer.

It was believed when someone received a cleansing, it washed away impurities or bad deeds and allowed the person to start a new life. The cleansing ceremony was performed by a priest and was followed with fasting and praying and other sacred practices.

When Five Killer had brought Maggie to the village last year, it was after the Green Corn Festival. This year, she felt the excitement the village experienced during the celebration.

"Has Awiagina spoken to Ayita about you and Oukonunaka?" Tayanita asked, winking at Galilani.

"No, why do you ask?" Maggie's eyes widened with feigned shock.

"You do not hide your feelings from me, sly fox," Tayanita replied.

Maggie stopped hoeing, speaking so none of the others overheard the conversation.

"I don't know how he feels about me. How did you know Mohe loved you?" Maggie asked, her eyes darted to see if anyone was listening.

"He told me, of course."

"I haven't talked to him about such things. But I did give him a kiss on his cheek when he helped me escape Boonesborough."

Both girls' eyes widened with surprise.

"You kissed Oukonunaka?" Galilani asked.

"I was so grateful for his helping me. He didn't say anything." Maggie was unsure what it meant. She was naive in the ways of such things as love.

"In time, he will talk about it," Tayanita said with a lilt in her voice.

Maggie sat on her pallet, Tracker lay on her lap, his leg twitched as he dreamed. She scratched his velvety belly.

Awiagina spoke from her bed. "Is there something wrong, Ahyoka? You have been quiet since returning from the field."

There was no use trying to hide her feelings. "Grandmother, I don't think Oukonunaka knows I care for him. He is older than me, maybe he thinks I'm just a little girl." Her face flamed, embarrassed to share her thoughts.

"Granddaughter, he doesn't know how you feel. A young warrior has to be told many things." She smiled, thinking to herself. "You must help him to know."

Maggie scratched Tracker's ear as he snuggled his nose into her skirt. She let Awiagina's words sink in.

The Green Corn Festival provided Maggie an opportunity to spend more time with Oukonunaka. She found him sitting with his friends outside the Council House. As she approached, his friends ignored her. Oukonunaka's conversation with the group of young braves ended abruptly.

"Hello, Ahyoka," he said, rising.

"Would you like to walk with me, Oukonunaka?"

The braves snickered, jabbing one another. Oukonunaka turned, giving a sharp retort to his friends.

"Yes, let's walk together." He led Ahyoka by the hand.

Maggie's heart fluttered against her chest. She hadn't held Oukonunaka's hand since he helped her escape from Boonesborough.

"Is the pup a good dog?" he asked.

"He is. Thank you for giving him to me." Maggie changed the subject. "Did you know Mohe and Tayanita are going to be marrying soon?"

"Yes, he brought a deer to her family this morning. Both grandmothers have given their consent," Oukonunaka said matter-of-factly.

"Tayanita's mother and father seem fond of Mohe."

Oukonunaka and Maggie walked to the edge of the woods and sat beneath a large sycamore tree. The crows cawed in the canopy of the forest, causing Maggie to speak louder than usual.

"I have been thinking about the journey to Boonesborough and the night I escaped."

"You were brave, Ahyoka." Oukonunaka pulled at a clump of grass. His eyes were fixed on the ground instead of Maggie.

"No, it was you who showed bravery. You waited all alone, watching out for me. You brought me home." She patted his hand. "You killed the wolf and protected me. I knew I . . . was fond of you that night."

"Ahyoka, in a few moons, I will be sixteen years." Oukonunaka felt his throat tighten and his palms felt like two fish. "I will be of age to find a girl to marry."

"Do you have someone in mind?" Maggie was afraid to hear the answer.

"Yes, I have thought about her every day for many days. I didn't know if she felt the same." He waited for Maggie to speak, lifting his eyes to hers.

"She does, Oukonunaka." Maggie took Awiagina's advice and quickly kissed his cheek. "I think of you every day, too."

Embarrassed for her bold move, Ahyoka rose from her place beside Oukonunaka and ran all the way back to her wigwam, not feeling her moccasins touch the ground.

Chapter 27

May 1778

Ahyoka celebrated her fifteenth birthday with the Cherokee tribe who had adopted her two years prior. Her use of English was reserved to her birch bark diaries that were kept in a wooden trunk Awiagina's husband brought back from a raid. Ahyoka wondered about the family who owned the trunk. It was given to her on her birthday a few days earlier.

Nanye'hi journeyed to different villages, encouraging the tribes to side with the colonists. She warned several settlements on the impending raids by the Cherokee.

Upon her return, Ahyoka listened with interest about the settlements she'd visited. After the Council House was emptied of the seven clans, Ahyoka approached the Beloved Woman.

"Nanye'hi, may I speak to you?" Ahyoka asked.

"Ahyoka, you speak our words well. What troubles you?" Nanye'hi read the anxious wringing of Ahyoka's hands.

"I wanted to ask if you saw any families who fled Boonesborough in the last two summers?"

"Are you asking for your white parents, Ahyoka?" She walked with her back to her wigwam as they conversed. "I spoke to the men of the villages. No women came to the meetings."

Ahyoka's spirit sank. She hadn't given up the hope she would be reunited with her mother, father, and brother. "They were said to have gone south to the Watauga area."

"Many settlers are raiding villages, killing old and young alike. To our south, our Cherokee brothers and sisters signed away the tribal villages through treaties the white men didn't keep."

"My father wouldn't take part in such killings. I'm sure of it." Ahyoka fiercely defended her father.

"The raids are like a snake, crawling toward our village, Ahyoka. We must decide whether to stay and fight the settlers or go further to the south."

Ahyoka thanked Nanye'hi for speaking with her. She'd hoped there would be some news of her family, but it looked unlikely they were still in the area.

"You are Cherokee now. We are your family, Ahyoka." Nanye'hi put her hands on her shoulders.

As she walked to her wigwam, she saw Tracker lying outside the door, waiting for her.

"Good boy, Tracker." She bent over to scratch the dog's neck. She sauntered down to the river's edge, Tracker walked along, his nose to the ground.

She saw Oukonunaka, Atohi, and Galegenoh climbing into their canoe and paddling away from the shore. She waved from her vantage point. She thought of their courtship over the year. He enjoyed teaching her the plants of the forest and how the Indians treated all parts of nature. Everything has a spirit, and she giggled at Oukonunaka thanking the fish he caught for giving up its life.

She taught him how to write his own name on birchbark. He learned to speak a bit of English in listening to Ahyoka read to him.

The Cherokee were aware of the dangers to the Indian villages as the War for Independence spread farther south. Ahyoka found herself worrying what would become of the tribe.

She sat on the bank with Tracker and watched the canoe carrying the three young warriors down the river. On this day, the river was calm, appearing as glass with the sun's rays illuminating its stillness. The canoe seemed to glide through the water without making a sound or ripple.

Her life with the Cherokee the last two years had seen Ahyoka grow into a young squaw. Awiagina's love and guidance provided Ahyoka the skills she needed to be a productive part of the village, as well as training her to be Oukonunaka's mate, should the two marry.

When the canoe rounded the bend, she brushed the grass from her skirt and called for Tracker, who had caught the scent of a rabbit and gave chase.

She walked back to her wigwam, Tracker bounded up the path to join her. As she walked, she noticed a pair of mourning doves searching for food underneath the ancient sycamore tree. They flew to a low branch as she passed them.

The men and women were busy in the gardens, taking care of the young plants. The squaws were carrying water by wooden buckets to give the plants a much-needed drink.

Overhead, Ahyoka saw a majestic hawk flying against the azure blue sky. The morning seemed perfect —the village buzzed with activity, then why did something feel amiss?

For most of the morning, Ahyoka helped the other squaws gather wild greens, mushrooms, and ramps from the forest. Her basket was full by the time they returned to the village. Her attention strayed to the river. Oukonunaka and the two other warriors hadn't returned yet, and she couldn't dismiss her uneasy feeling.

Ahyoka kneaded the acorn flour dough into a round loaf. She placed the loaf on a stone inside the brick oven. While the bread baked, she helped Tayanita and Galilani wash and cut the greens and mushrooms. The scent of the ramps filled her nostrils, causing her eyes to water. The wild onions were plentiful after the good rainfall earlier in the week.

"How is Meho getting along with your family, Tayanita?" Ahyoka asked, reaching for another clump of ramps.

"My father and Meho are hunting together. I think he is happy to have a son now."

"You will be married one day soon as well, Ahyoka." Tayanita and Galilani smiled at one another. They knew there were strong feelings between Ahyoka and Oukonunaka.

"I am happy knowing he cares for me, I am too young for marrying," Maggie said in a frivolous manner.

"Where is Oukonunaka? I didn't see him when Meho went with my father."

"Atohi, Galegenoh, and Oukonunaka took the canoe out on the river." Ahyoka said and rushed to the oven to retrieve the baked bread. "I've been . . .," she searched for the word she wanted to say, "worried."

She heard the whoop almost as soon as the word left her mouth. She dropped the rag in her hand and bolted down the hill, jumping over rocks and tree roots. She slid, almost losing her balance and tumbling headlong down the embankment to the river.

By the time she reached the bank, several others were making their way down to join her. The canoe was being paddled by Galegenoh. Ahyoka's heart was in her throat. She didn't see Oukonunaka or Atohi.

She wrung her hands as Galegenoh reached the water's edge. He jumped into the river to pull the canoe onto the bank. Lying inside, slumped over on their sides, was Oukonunaka and Atohi. Blood covered the floor of the canoe.

Ahyoka screamed, frozen in place. Oukonunaka's aunt, Ayita, began wailing when she saw her nephew's condition. A dozen thoughts rushed through Ahyoka's mind.

What had happened to the trio?

"Galegenoh, what happened?" Ayita asked, helping the other squaws lift the two warriors from the canoe. Five Killer came over the bank in time to see the two young men being carried up to the shade of the willow tree.

"Where did this happen?" Five Killer barked.

"We were near the cane breaks. We went to cut cane for blow guns." Galegenoh's voice was weak, his muscles ached from rowing as quickly as he could.

Five Killer hurried up the bank, half-dragging Galegenoh up the hill to the village.

The women began searching for bullet wounds on the two warriors. Upon closer inspection, Atohi's shoulder was almost blown from his body. The bullet had shattered his shoulder blade and he was losing blood in an astonishing amount.

Ahyoka felt Awiagina's arms encircle her, pulling her back from the ghastly scene.

"Come with me, Granddaughter. We will make bandages and carry clean water." She took Ahyoka to her wigwam. She didn't see Oukonunaka's wound. The bullet passed through his chest under his collarbone.

The Chief came to see who had been attacked, and upon seeing the two young warriors, instructed a band of warriors to prepare to attack the nearby settlement.

Galegenoh explained the three were in the cane break cutting the stalks, when Oukonunaka spotted the tricorn hat from across the break. Galegenoh motioned with his hands to explain the hat.

The three took off to the river bank, but the white settler shot twice. Atohi dropped to the ground, but Oukonunaka and Galegenoh dragged him to the canoe. The white settler was dragging a large doe to his horse, he had no bullets left or he would have shot Galegenoh.

By the time Awiagina and Ahyoka returned, a patch of crimson formed where Atohi's body lay. The medicine man, Yonaguska, had the men carrying both warriors to his wigwam.

The warriors began applying the war paint to their faces and body. The red and black paint gave a terrifying impression to the receiving end of their raid.

Atohi's condition was grave, having lost a large amount of blood, not to mention his mangled shoulder. The medicine man poured a dark drink into a gourd dipper. His mother, Leotie, cradled his head on her lap as he slipped into darkness.

Awiagina and Ahyoka entered the medicine man's wigwam, carrying hot pots of water and many clean bandages. Ahyoka crouched beside Oukonunaka. She noted the pain in his eyes.

The medicine man applied yarrow, a fragrant plant, in the form of a poultice, hoping to stop the blood flow from Oukonunaka's wound. He also hoped it would clot the blood in Atohi's mangled shoulder.

"Grandmother, will he live?" Ahyoka whispered.

"Only the Great Spirit decides such things, Ahyoka." She looked at the medicine man, knowing Atohi's condition was grave.

Ahyoka put her head on Awiagina's shoulder. Oukonunaka was given sips of a dark liquid from a small gourd. He tried raising his head, but the task proved difficult.

She knelt beside him, and whispered into his ear, "I love you, brave warrior."

Chapter 28

The following morning, Atohi's body was prepared for burial. The loss of blood and the condition of his shoulder proved more than the medicine man, or his poultice, could heal.

A gentle breeze blew the leaves as if to wave farewell to the young warrior. The night of Atohi's death, several of the men of the village went to the burial ground and dug a hole for the body. Two warriors were placed to guard the hole so that no bad spirits entered.

A solemn procession carried Atohi's cloth wrapped body out of the village. Everyone came out to support the young warrior, and Ahyoka walked in the procession of mourners to the burial site. The Chief spoke words and said prayers over the body.

Atohi's mother and other family members were now in mourning.

They wore dirt on their faces and hair and didn't cleanse for seven days. The mourning period would last several months.

After the burial, Ahyoka and Awiagina remained silent as they made their way from the burial ground to the village.

Once they reached the Council House, they saw warriors preparing to leave. Ahyoka knew they would be killing settlers and burning their villages in retaliation for the attack on Atohi, Oukonunaka, and Galegenoh.

Their painted bodies and faces gave Ahyoka chills. She worried about the families in the wake of the terror they were about to receive. Her heart was saddened, but she knew this was justice in the eyes of the Cherokee.

Just as she was brought to the village to avenge the death of Little Bear's daughter and husband, someone would lose their life to avenge the death of Atohi.

Thankful that Oukonunaka would not die from his wound, she wanted the man who shot him and Atohi to be killed. She didn't want to think about condoning a murder, but, she was angry and wanted retribution for Oukonunaka.

The warriors left the village carrying war clubs, bows and arrows, and rifles. Nanye'hi feared the whites would return to attack their village, as they had done to the village of her uncle and cousin, Dragging Canoe. The Red Chief led the warriors out the village doors in a triumphant war whoop.

Ahyoka walked to Oukonunaka's wigwam and waited for his uncle, Atsadi, to allow her entrance. She squinted, giving her eyes time to adjust to the low light. Oukonunaka lay on a bed of animal skins, his eyes closed. His shoulder was covered in a medicine poultice to aid healing of the wound. A gourd filled with dark liquid sat on the floor beside him.

"Is he better today?" she whispered, not wanting to disturb him.

"The Great Spirit watches over Oukonunaka. His spirit is stronger this morning."

Hearing Ahyoka's voice, Oukonunaka's eyelids fluttered. He slowly turned his head and opened his eyes to see her kneeling beside him.

"I saw you in the cane . . . you warned me." His eyes closed again.

Ahyoka looked up at his uncle. She wondered what he meant.

"I was here all the time, with Awiagina, but I prayed for your safe return."

Feeling the effects of the drink from the medicine man, Oukonunaka fell into a deep sleep.

"You are good medicine for my nephew, Ahyoka," Atsadi said as he walked with her outside. His wife, Ayita, sat on the floor beside Oukonunaka and finished a pair of moccasins.

Ahyoka left the wigwam. The sun's rays cast golden beams across the village. The smell of cooking fires filled her nose, along with the smell of bean bread wafting from the domed oven.

She met Tayanita carrying a basket of roasting ears to be shucked for the afternoon meal.

"How is Oukonunaka this morning?" She shielded the bright sunlight from her eyes.

"He seems better, thanks be to God." She turned and joined her friend.

Tayanita nodded, "Yes, the Great Spirit watches over Oukonunaka. He will be chief one day."

Ahyoka learned after her return to the village that Oukonunaka's uncle and aunt were of his deceased mother's clan. His grandfather was Yonaguska, Red Chief, one of the war chiefs.

After the death of his father and mother, Oukonunaka's uncle and aunt took him and his sisters in. With no son, Yonaguska's grandson will one day take his place as chief, if the Council agrees.

Tayanita sat in front of her family's wigwam and stripped the husk from the corn. The Green Corn Festival would soon be celebrated. Even though it was an exciting time for the Cherokee, a feeling of uncertainty hung as a shroud, waning the excitement. Tayanita and Mohe were expecting their first child. She would give birth sometime in the fall.

Awiagina was busy skinning and dressing the two rabbits she was given by her nephew, Wohali. She always received meat whenever Wohali hunted. His aunt was now his only aunt still living, and he would look after her as if she were his own mother.

The warriors kept a watchful eye as the rest of the village went about their daily routines. Tayanita's husband, Meho, and the other warriors hadn't returned from their raiding party.

Oukonunaka awoke to see his aunt smiling at him.

"You had a visitor, nephew." Ayita's eyes went back to the moccasins and the task athand.

"How is Atohi? Does he live?" Oukonunaka tried raising from his pallet.

"Lie still, you are as weak as a newborn fawn." She gently pushed him back to his pallet.

"Does he live?" he asked, his voice becoming more demanding.

"No, he was buried two days ago." Her sympathetic eyes cast a lone tear down her cheek.

"I must avenge his death." He tried to rise from the pallet.

"No, Oukonunaka. It is being done, and you must get well."

He turned his face from his aunt, the tears for his friend and brother soaked the rabbit skin under his face.

Chapter 29

The month of August followed a period of heat and drought in the villages near the Owotee River. It also brought back the warriors and the news of the attacks on settlers living around the salt licks and settlements of Boonesborough. The death of Atohi was now avenged. Two prisoners, both male, were tied together and dragged into the village. The journey from Boonesborough and settlements to the mountains lasted for three weeks. The warriors, numbering over thirty returned with twenty-two warriors and two captives.

The entire village sat inside the Council House where the proud warriors told of the retribution brought to the settlers. In doing so, they recounted the loss of each warrior. The warriors' families cry of sorrow lifted to the rafters of the Council House.

Tayanita and her young warrior husband, Mohe, were reunited once again. Sitting with the Long Hair clan, he held up his coup stick to Oukonunaka, who was sitting with the Deer clan.

Oukonunaka and Galegenoh called out as the attack on the hunter was described. His scalp, tied to a coup stick, was presented to Oukonunaka. He raised the scalp into the air, with Galegenoh and others joining in a chorus of whoops and cheers.

The two captives, tied together, stood, terrified as to what would befall them. Ahyoka found herself not feeling the compassion for the men as she would have two years before.

It was decided the men would be tied to two large poles in the center of the village. Everyone carried limbs and small logs of wood to heap upon the pile. The men called out for someone to spare them. It was up to Nanye'hi, the Beloved Woman, to either grant their executions or pardon them.

Known for her compassion for prisoners, Nanye'hi chose to allow the executions. Amid the pleas and cries of the prisoners, the brush piles were lit. The gruesome ritual was more than Ahyoka could stomach. She was thankful the prisoners were not the settlers she knew from Boonesborough, even though they were someone's family. She tried to put their cries out of her mind as she went back to her wigwam. When she reached the door, she heard her name and turned to see Oukonunaka walking toward her.

"You know they will keep attacking our villages if we don't stop them," he said.

"I don't understand why we are fighting. I don't understand why the British are fighting us, I mean, the colonists. Why do we have to have war? Isn't there enough land for all of us?" Ahyoka's anger surprised Oukonunaka.

"The English and the settlers all have taken what is not theirs. Our people have signed treaties- they are worth nothing! They take and take and take some more. Now they want to take the lives of our people." Oukonunaka stopped, his voice drowning out the screams coming from the dying captives.

"My father and mother, Little Bear and Degataga, Woya, Chea Sequa, and Atohi. all killed by settlers."

"I know. I think of my mother, father, and brother. Where are they and what has become of them?"

"Someday, I believe you will know." Oukonunaka reached out his hand, "Come, walk with me."

Oukonunaka led Ahyoka away from the torture and death taking place near the Council House. They went to the bank of the river where he stopped her from running away two years earlier.

He'd whittled a small owl from a broken river birch branch and handed it to her.

"Do you know what my name means, Ahyoka?"

"Yes, since I have learned more of your words. It means White Owl." She smiled, taking the wooden figure, turning it over in her hands to marvel at the work.

"This will protect you, like the owl that protected us from the wolves." He reminded her of the owl that alerted them during their return to the village.

"I love the gift, thank you." She felt embarrassed because she had nothing to give in return.

"Now that I am returning to health, I wanted to thank you. This is my gift of thanks."

"I don't understand." Ahyoka's eyebrows scrunched together.

"You warned me to run from the canebrake. I heard your voice. It was before the hunter shot Atohi and me. If I hadn't been alerted, he would have killed us all."

Ahyoka remembered their conversation the day she visited him. When he opened his eyes, he said she'd called out to him. His uncle heard the words too.

"I prayed for your safety, Oukonunaka."

"Ahyoka, I have thought about the signs, and I have prayed to the Great Spirit each morning at dawn for His guidance."

Ahyoka swallowed the lump rising in her throat. "Guidance, Oukonunaka?"

"I have spoken to my uncle and aunt. They have given me their blessing. Now I must speak to Awiagina." He looked into her questioning eyes, taking her hand in his. "I want you to be my wife."

Chapter 30

The question hit Ahyoka like a lead weight. He wanted to marry her, a girl of fifteen winters.

If she lived in Boonesborough, or back home in Culpeper, her mother and father would have said no. But they weren't here, and life among the Cherokee was different than with the white settlers.

With the War for Independence dragging on another year and settlers raiding Cherokee settlements, a long life was not a guarantee. Oukonunaka and Ahyoka's marriage would depend on Awiagina.

Awiagina sat under the cool shade of the ancient willow tree. Her wrinkled hands expertly weaved the hickory bark and honeysuckle vine into the beginning of a beautiful basket. She looked up as Oukonunaka led Ahyoka to speak with her.

"Ahyoka, you must do something with your dog. He ate the bread I had cooling on the rock outside my door."

"I'm sorry, Grandmother. After the meeting at the Council House, I forgot to tie him to the post beside our wigwam. I was distracted." Ahyoka gave Tracker a stern look.

"You both look like the doe before she is brought down with an arrow. What is on your minds?" She acted unaware, even though she suspected the reason for their serious faces.

"Awiagina, I've spoken with my uncle and aunt." His throat felt like he was chewing on a tuft of sheep's wool. "I want to speak with you," he started to lose his nerve.

Awiagina put down the basket she was working on and patted the log on either side of her. "Both of you, sit."

Oukonunaka and Ahyoka did as they were told. Awiagina took their hands in hers.

"When I was your age, Granddaughter, my Cheveyo spoke with my father and mother. I was but a young girl, an innocent blossom on the honeysuckle vine. And Cheveyo was three winters older than me." Her hands could feel the shaking in each of their hands. "But my father knew Cheveyo would take care of me. So, he came to live with my family in our wigwam. We were only married a year before he was killed by the Creek."

Ahyoka's eyes widened as if wondering where Awiagina was going with her speech. Oukonunaka was silent, listening to the elder woman. Awiagina turned to Oukonunaka.

"Oukonunaka, you have the chance to become a great chief for our people. You have a good spirit." She squeezed his hand, now wet with sweat.

"Ahyoka, you are young, as I was, but you have shown your love for our people, becoming one of us and returning to live among us. There is talk of our village moving away from Coyatee. Too many whites and many raids on our people. Ahyoka, you will need protection when I'm gone."

Ahyoka didn't want to think of losing Awiagina, the woman she loved almost as much as her own mother.

"So, I give you my blessing. We will begin preparing for you to move into our wigwam. But first, you must bring me a doe or bear for the winter. We will need meat for the winter."

She smiled, revealing the four teeth she had left in her mouth. Both Oukonunaka and Ahyoka hugged Awiagina and thanked her.

"I will speak to Nanye'hi and my grandfather. Thank you, Awiagina."

"You may call me Grandmother, Oukonunaka."

He nodded and ran off to find his grandfather, the Chief.

"Thank you, Grandmother."

"I will begin working on a new dress for you." She picked up the basket and walked with a slow gait to her wigwam. "Come, granddaughter. We must have a talk now that you are to be a wife." Awiagina didn't know if Ahyoka's white mother had spoken about such things to her when she received her monthly flow.

"Grandmother, when will we move to the south?"

"Nanye'hi has visited her uncle in the settlement on the Holston river. We will join with the people there, away from the fighting. This land is stained with the blood of our people.

Ahyoka worried about the words Awiagina spoke. What else was there to know about being a wife? She loved Oukonunaka, and he would protect her now. Something else weighed on her mind. If the village had to move, they would need to move before the winter snow arrived. Ahyoka remembered their trek into Kentucke. It would be a dangerous journey.

Ahyoka followed her grandmother inside the wigwam. She went back to her pallet and removed a section of birch bark from her trunk.

With a piece of sharpened wood and the ink she'd made from blackberry juice, she wrote:

August 1778, Oukonunaka asked Grandmother for her blessing for our wedding.

"Granddaughter did your white mother speak to you about your duty as a wife?" she searched for understanding in Ahyoka's eyes.

Ahyoka's cheeks turned crimson. "Yes, she spoke of such things the summer before I was taken captive." She lowered her eyes, "I know what is expected. Tayanita shared with me what happens when the husband comes to our wigwam."

Awiagina smiled. "Good. You and I must begin work on your wedding dress."

In late August, the village saw more warriors leave to join the fighting on the side of the British. Nanye'hi warned two settlements of impending attacks by her cousin, Dragging Canoe.

The Overhill Cherokee saw more attacks by British led settlers to remove them from the area. Virginia militia sent troops to wipe out the villages in the eastern portion of the Cherokee nation. Nanye'hi and the Chiefs decided to move the village further south to avoid conflicts with the settlers.

During September, the attacks struck towns to the south of Coyatee. It was decided to leave before the snow arrived in the late fall. The tribe would join other Cherokee in the capital town of Chota.

Ahyoka and Oukonunaka would be allowed to marry before the journey. The wedding preparations took three weeks from the time Oukonunaka spoke to his aunt and Awiagina. His grandfather took longer to give his blessing. He thought the young warrior should look for a Cherokee woman for his wife but found no fault in Ahyoka. Seeing his grandson's resolve, he granted his blessing.

In the Cherokee society, clanship is matrilineal. It is forbidden to marry within one's own clan. Because the woman holds the family clan, she is represented at the ceremony by both her mother, or clan mother if her mother is deceased, and her oldest brother. Since Ahyoka had no mother or brother, Awiagina represented her, along with Awiagina's nephew, Waya. On September 12th, 1778, Ahyoka and Oukonunaka began the marriage rituals.

Waya stood with a nervous Ahyoka as he gave his vow to take the responsibility of teaching the children in spiritual and religious matters, as that is the traditional role of the uncle—*e-du-tsi*.

Ahyoka and Oukonunaka met at the center of the Council House, and the groom gave the bride a ham of venison while she gave an ear of corn to him, then the wedding party danced and feasted for hours.

In those early days, venison symbolized the groom's intention to keep meat in the household and the corn symbolized the bride's willingness to be a good Cherokee housewife. The groom was accompanied by his aunt, Ayita.

After the sacred setting for the ceremony had been blessed for seven consecutive days, it was time for the ceremony. Ahyoka and Oukonunaka approached the sacred fire and the Beloved Woman blessed them. All participants in the wedding, including the guests, were also blessed. Songs were sung in Cherokee, and those conducting the ceremony blessed the couple. Both the Ahyoka and Oukonunaka were each covered in a blue blanket. At a specific moment in the ceremony, the Beloved Woman removed each blue blanket, and covered the couple with one white blanket, indicating the beginning of their new life together.

Instead of exchanging rings, as in a Christian ceremony, the couple exchanged food. Oukonunaka brought ham of venison to indicate his intention to provide for the household. Ahyoka provided bean bread to symbolize her willingness to care for and provide nourishment for her household.

Next, the couple drank together from a Cherokee wedding vase. The vessel held one drink but had two openings for the couple to drink from at the same time. Following the ceremony, the clans of both families provided a wedding feast, and the dancing and celebrating continued all through the night and into the next morning.

The marriage ceremony was nothing like Ahyoka had witnessed in Culpeper or Boonesborough. She thought of her parents and her brother during the week of wedding celebration. Even though her heart was full, a small part of her happiness was missing.

After the wedding meal, Nanye'hi gave Ahyoka a gift: a quill pen with ink and a pewter inkwell. Her white husband traded beads and pottery with a southern Tory family the last time he visited Coyatee.

Ahyoka thanked Nanye'hi, wrapping her arms around the Beloved Woman. It had been three years since she'd written with ink. She treasured the gift and wouldn't have to use blackberry juice or the ink from boiled walnuts to write on the birch bark. She longed for real paper but would someday make a trade when close to friendly settlers.

After the festivities ended, Ahyoka and Oukonunaka retired to the wigwam they shared with Awiagina. They heard the cheers outside the door as they blew out the pine knot candle lighting the room and began their married life together.

Chapter 31

October 1778

The squirrels gathered nuts, poking them into their jowls, as the travois were being loaded with possessions from the now empty wigwams and summer houses.

Ahyoka helped with the last of Tayanita's blankets and pots, as she was at least with a month left in her pregnancy. Mohe and Oukonunaka tied their possessions down to the blanket of hides with buffalo tugs.

Five Killer spoke to the warriors about keeping their rifles, bows and arrows, and other weapons on their person at all times. The British and colonists were waging war closer to the mountains, and there might be troops of soldiers in the area.

Ahyoka and Tayanita exchanged apprehensive looks. With her baby due to arrive in another month, travel over the rough terrain could be dangerous for her and the baby.

Dogs were tethered to the travois', and the warriors who'd returned from fighting brought several horses. Awiagina was allowed a horse to ride. Ahyoka led the horse and Oukonunaka walked beside the travois pulled by the now mature dogs, Tracker and Tsaladihi.

The journey would take at least a week of traveling down river to Chota. Before departing, prayers for protection were given to the tribe. Ahyoka took one last look as they walked away. Several warriors carried their canoes to the river where they would join the tribe downstream.

The stiff autumn wind swirled the falling leaves of orange, red, and gold against the gray sky. Soon, the dry leaves would cover the ground, making their approach in the forest more difficult to conceal. Squirrels barked their fare-thee-wells to the men, women, and children. Over two hundred left the village on that day, along with their horses, dogs and travois carrying all they possessed.

Many in the tribe were leaving behind the only village they'd ever known. There were Indians from the Shawnee and Delaware tribes who were part of the Cherokee village. These Indians had been adopted into the tribe, as had Ahyoka.

Ahyoka understood their tears. They were tears filled with the same emotions she had upon leaving her stone and wood house in Culpeper. Instead of the young girl who traveled through The Gap with Daniel Boone, she was now the wife of the proud warrior, Oukonunaka.

She prayed their new village would keep them safe from the attacks of the frontier settlers. They would remain at Chota for the time being. Already the Cherokee had given up most of their lands in the Overhill portion of the Cherokee Nation. The tribal chiefs disagreed on how best to keep their lands without continuing to wage war against the settlers.

The journey to Chota was most difficult on the very young and very old. Children became sick from the cold. Awiagina gave up the horse, saying it bounced her bones against one another something fierce.

Ahyoka walked with her, holding on to her hand, while in her other hand she carried a hickory walking stick. Seeing Tayanita walking slower than Awiagina, she called to her when they stopped to rest and eat some from the provisions they carried in their packs.

"Are you well, Tayanita?" Ahyoka asked.

"I'm well," she replied, but her face showed otherwise.

Awiagina joined Tayanita's mother, Inola, and the other squaw. Ahyoka knew they were discussing Tayanita and her condition.

During the rest, it was clear she wasn't well at all. The women discussed the possibility they would need to stop along the way to deliver Tayanita's child.

November 12, 1778

The tribe reached Chota on the last day of October, seven days after leaving Coyatee. Tayanita delivered a son, and as was the custom, her mother named the child Tsali.

Upon their arrival, arrangements were made for the families to be housed with other families until living quarters were built.

Ahyoka and Oukonunaka shared a home with Awiagina, her nephew, his wife, and two daughters.

Their living space consisted of one large room with a fire pit in the center of the room. There was a small loft overhead where items could be stored.

The sweat house, or winter house, resembled an upside-down basket. Like their homes in Coyatee, the occupants remained dry and warm with the fire burning. With no chimney for the smoke to escape, the room appeared cloudy and had an overpowering smell of wood smoke.

The new residents of Chota hurried to construct homes of their own. As soon as the wood and vines were cut, a new winter home of wattle and daub was constructed. Many hands worked together to build these structures as quick as possible. Winter snow and colder temperatures would soon be upon them.

The Council House was as large as anything she'd seen since coming to the wilderness. Easily seating five hundred Indians, the clans took their places around the arbor. The chiefs assembled, along with Nanye'hi. Oukonunaka's grandfather spoke harshly to Dragging Canoe, who attacked settlements in Watauga. Ahyoka listened as the chiefs spoke of the traders who lived in the village. Some of the traders had Cherokee wives.

She would visit the one called Josiah Klumpf, a German who'd immigrated to Philadelphia, but left soon after the war broke out. A Quaker, he was a pacifist.

She wanted to make a trade for more ink and a new quill tip. She filled two whole sheets writing about her wedding and the gifts the tribe brought.

The meeting ended, catching Ahyoka daydreaming. Awiagina nudged her with her bony elbow. She sat straight on the bench. Ahyoka followed her out of the Council House.

Oukonunaka and his uncle hurried to work on their sweat house. Ahyoka went to work grinding hickory nuts in a wooden kanona—a hollowed out stump a few inches in depth. A large heavy stick of wood was used as a pestle to pound the nuts into a consistency to be placed in a ball. The balls must be kept in a cool, dry place until ready to use. The nuts had been gathered from the hickory trees at Cayotee and dried several weeks prior to pounding.

Awiagina sat in front of a large stone with a mallet and pounded the shells to reveal the nuts inside. These were sifted through a basket twice, then handed over to Ahyoka to grind.

They were planning on making a delicacy to the Cherokee called kanuchi. The ball of hickory nut meat would be crumbled into a pot of boiling water and stirred until the mixture would be strained through a cloth to remove the pieces of shell, then returned to boil. If there was any rice to be had, it would be added into the slurry mixture. Honey would also be added before eating. The concoction was a favorite and would be eaten throughout the year as a soup.

Oukonunaka especially loved it, and it was being prepared for his eighteenth birthday. After she finished her job with the hickory nuts, she hurried off alone to visit Josiah Klumpf's tent to see if there was something she might make a trade for Oukonunaka's gift.

She took a quick glance back where the men were working on the wattle and daub dwelling. Seeing no one noticed, she slipped into the tent to have a look at Mr. Klumpf's wears.

Ahyoka spoke to Mr. Klumpf in English. "Good day, Mr. Klumpf."

He seemed surprised to hear such good English from the Cherokee girl, until he looked closer. "Good day, and how are you this fine day?"

Ahyoka smiled, it reminded her of home hearing someone speaking her native language fluently. "I'm well, thank you. I would like to find something for my husband's birthday. I have a basket that I could trade." She brought forth a small basket made of birch bark. It was simple, but well-made.

"Let me have a look-see." He turned the basket over and back again, noticing the tightness in her weave. "My missus would be mighty proud to have this fine basket by such a young lady." He removed his cap, smoothed his unruly curls, then replaced the cap. "Pardon my forwardness, but are you one of the captives here in the village?"

Ahyoka kept her eyes down as she picked up a pocket watch similar to the one her father kept on a fob in his vest.

"I was taken some years ago from Boonesborough but was given my freedom when the woman who adopted me was killed by settlers. When I returned to Boonesborough, my parents and several of the people who came with us from Virginia were gone."

She looked Mr. Klumpf square in the eyes. She didn't feel sorry for herself, she was thankful for the love of the Cherokee who'd made her part of their tribe. She handed the watch back to him.

"That is quite a tale, young lady," Mr. Klumpf said. He put the watch back in the tray of finery.

Ahyoka spied a rectangular box and a small knife. The knife was a Barlow knife, teardrop shaped with a horn bolster, perfect for Oukonunaka's whittling. It would be a perfect gift.

"Would you make a trade . . . this knife for my basket?"

"I got that knife from a settler in Watauga settlement. It might be worth two baskets." Mr. Klumpf was a shrewd trader.

"May I see the wooden box, please?" She found the small rectangular box interesting, and well-made.

"That box was made by a fine carpenter from Watauga settlement, last winter."

Ahyoka held the slide-lid box with its delicate carving on the lid. She turned the box over, seeing a familiar mark on the bottom. JD 1777.

"Do you remember the carpenter's name who traded this box?" Ahyoka's voice rose with excitement.

"Well, now, he said he came to the frontier by way of Culp . . ."

Ahyoka interrupted him, "Culpeper?"

"Yes, a good Christian man. He made this for my son," he said, digging in his personal box of possessions. He lifted a small sling shot, identical to her brother Will's.

"Oh my. This is my father's work. He made one for my brother and the boys in Boonesborough. This box, it has his mark: JD, Jacob Diele." Ahyoka's eyes filled with tears as she ran her fingers over the box. She imagined her father with his carving tools working on the box.

"What's your Christian name, girl?" he asked.

"Maggie Diele. My parents, Jacob and Christena Diele, and my brother Wilhelm, left Boonesborough after they thought I was killed by the Indians." Ahyoka wiped her eyes with her hand.

"Merciful heaven, child. Are you sure this is your father's work?"

"Quite so. I have seen him add his mark. This is my father's."

"You must have it. It is Providence that brought you to it." He handed the box to Ahyoka, who held it as if it would break.

"I don't know how to thank you. Tell me, were they well?" Ahyoka found her wits and wanted to know more about her parents.

"I didn't see anyone else, just your father. I'm sorry, child." He handed her the Barlow knife in a leather pouch. "I plan on going back to Virginia when the war ends. I would be proud to tell Mr. Diele you are well, if I see him again."

"Thank you. I will bring your basket." Ahyoka put the box and pouch with the knife into her pack. "Before you go back to Virginia, would you carry a letter for me?"

"Yes, I plan on going back to trade with the settlements along the Nolichucky, barring no British soldiers or Creek go on the war path." He didn't mean to disrespect her but felt bad for saying it just the same.

"Good day, Mr. Klumpf, and thank you." Ahyoka left the tent with a renewed hope. Her parents were alive, at least as of the last winter. The attacks by Dragging Canoe earlier in the year hadn't taken their lives.

She took her possessions into the wigwam where Awiagina spun the wool she'd brought from Coyatee. The animals were still in pens near the dwellings, as well as the cows and horses.

"Grandmother, I have wonderful news." Ahyoka hurried to tell Awiagina what she'd learned from the trader.

Her nephew was working on a home, as were the other men, leaving his wife and daughters to work inside. They were sewing skirts from the material they purchased with deer skins.

As Ahyoka retold the story, they listened as she showed them first the box, then the Barlow knife for Oukonunaka's birthday gift.

"You made a good trade, Ahyoka," Leoti said, admiring the knife.

"Yes, it was a good trade, but I have my father's work and they are at Watauga Settlement. That is not far, is it?"

"It is several weeks over mountains," she said.

Ahyoka had no plans of running away. She loved Oukonunaka and didn't want to leave him. Awiagina needed her as well. She resigned herself to believe she would see her family again.

That evening, Ahyoka gave the knife to Oukonunaka. He examined the fine detail in the bolster. "Thank you, Ahyoka. It is a fine gift." He kissed her, in front of the family members gathered in the wigwam. "Tomorrow our wigwam will be ready, and we will start on the next."

Ahyoka settled into her warm bed of fur and deer skin with Oukonunaka.

Chapter 32

December 1778

Two traders moving through the mountains wandered into the village, two days before Christmas. They brought with them an ox cart wagon packed with supplies. Edward Garrett and Thomas Macleod spoke of the British taking the city of Savannah to the south in the colony of Georgia. They also told the chiefs of Chota about attacks by the Indians with British guns in the South Carolina upcountry.

Ahyoka wondered if they had been to the Watauga settlement. Her parents were there the year before. She wondered, were they still living there? Nanye'hi had warned the settlers of the attack by Dragging Canoe, saving hundreds.

The Beloved Woman and the two traders spoke at length about other attacks on the surrounding settlements. As a Peace Chief, she tried warning the settlers of attacks when possible. Mayhap in the spring, Ahyoka could accompany Nanye'hi to the settlement.

Mr. Macleod also told of North Carolina opening settlements in Washington county. Areas once belonging to the Cherokee had been ceded to the state. More and more of the Cherokee lands were taken, causing Dragging Canoe and his warriors to raid and attack the settlements from South Carolina to Kentucke.

On Christmas Eve, Ahyoka wrote in her journal of the two men who came into their village.

24 December 1778~ On this night a heavy snow covered our village. Oukonunaka has made two doves with the whittling knife. He looks different now that he is completely shaven, except for the topknot. A turkey feather is worn on a band around his head. His nose is pierced with a metal ring and his ear fashions the same. My protector.

He gave me a silver bracelet which I will never remove. On this night, I remember Papa reading the story of the blessed birth. I retold them the story as Papa read it from the Bible, the birth of Christ in the manger.

The ink well was almost dry. Her pen would remain silent until she could trade for more ink with the men who were unable to leave until spring.

On Christmas morning, Oukonunaka worked to open the wigwam door. Awiagina didn't stir from her pallet as he wrapped himself in a wool blanket and went out to give morning prayers to the Great Spirit.

Ahyoka warmed a bowl of kanuchi over the fire. The wigwam was warm, it's wattle and daub walls were tight. She was proud of her husband. The work to build the wigwam was warrior's work, but the dwelling belonged to the squaw.

"Good morning, Grandmother. Would you like a bowl of kanuchi with bear bacon?" Ahyoka cut a chunk off and added it to the iron skillet over the fire. She traded four baskets for the skillet.

"Yes, thank you, Granddaughter. My bones are cold this morning."

The women, with blankets wrapped around their shoulders, ate their breakfast.

Oukonunaka came through the door, covered in snow. Tracker's tail thumped against the dirt floor, excited to see a deer's antler in Oukonunaka's hand.

"Here, chew on something besides my moccasin." He pretended to be angry with the dog. The deer antler was taken to Tracker's spot in the wigwam where he gnawed in happiness.

"We will have full stomachs thanks to the venison you brought back on your hunt before the snow fell." Ahyoka lifted the bacon from the skillet.

"I spoke to Mohe this morning. He tells me Tsali is not well," Oukonunaka said, taking a bite of kanuchi.

"Grandmother, can you make some tea from the squirrel tail plant? It might do him well if Tayanita drinks and passes it to him." Ahyoka believed in the healing power of herbs and the plants of the forest. The birth of Tsali along the way to Chota gave the infant a difficult start to life. The rain and cold of the journey took its toll on the vulnerable.

"I will go with you, Grandmother," said Ahyoka.

After they finished preparing the tea, Awiagina and Ahyoka put on their moccasin boots and walked through the snow—now up to their calves—to visit the wigwam of Mohe and Tayanita.

The child slept in a small cradle lined with rabbit fur and wrapped in a heavy blanket.

Ahyoka touched the child's cheek, cool and yellow. The jaundiced condition was caused by a liver malady, fatal to an infant.

Tsali had already been visited by the medicine man of the tribe, and neither parent wanted to believe their beloved infant would not awaken from his slumber.

Awiagina and Ahyoka offered their prayers and words of comfort to the parents before leaving them to their vigil.

"My heart is sad for Tayanita. He won't come back to health will he, Grandmother?"

"It is the decision of the Great Spirit. Only the mountains live forever, child."

The cruel fact of death on the frontier was common for the Cherokee and pioneers. Tsali lived but a few hours after Ahyoka and Awiagina said prayers over the infant. The winter snow lasted for weeks in the mountains, bringing sickness and death to those already weak from other ailments.

The fighting in the south and north proved successful for the British. Vincennes was captured once again in the north, and to the south, Savannah fell to British forces on December 29th.

Word of the war came slowly to the village of Chota. Ahyoka penned a letter to her parents and walked through the snow to deliver it to Mr. Klumpf. He planned to leave the settlement and travel east, passing through the Watauga region.

The rest of the winter, the village survived on what food stores they had in their wigwams and by hunting the game that came near caves. Saltpeter was discovered two days south of the village near the mouth of a large cave in the hillside. They no longer needed to make the trip into Kentucke.

Oukonunaka, along with Mohe, Tsiyi, Galegenoh, and four other warriors, left to hunt the game that gathered near the licks.

They would be gone for a week, traveling down the Tennessee River to the river bend. From there, the warriors would carry their canoes and baskets a day's walk into the mountains to the salt lick.

On the morning of his departure, Oukonunaka went to the edge of the village to pray. When he returned, Ahyoka met him at the river's edge. Wrapped in a buffalo robe, she shivered as the raw wind lifted her loose hair, not yet braided. She touched his cheek, wanting to leave her warmth on his face. The gray sky hid the sun's rays, causing the temperature to feel even colder than it was. He pulled his blanket around his shoulders.

"Come back to me, my handsome warrior." She burrowed into his chest.

"The Great Owl will travel with me, and I have your touch to keep me warm." He touched first his cheek and then his heart.

The warriors departed, their canoes gliding quietly on the river. The cold caused Ahyoka to shiver and pull her buffalo robe tightly around her. She spent the rest of the afternoon with Tayanita in her wigwam. The two friends hadn't seen much of one another since Tayanita's son was buried.

"Why don't you join Grandmother and me until Mohe and Oukonunaka return? I would enjoy your company," Ahyoka offered. She knew Tayanita would rather keep company with someone of her own age, instead of her parents and her mother's widowed sister.

"If Awiagina is agreeable to it, I would very much like to stay with you."

"Grandmother hasn't been feeling herself the past few days. I think you would be good medicine for her."

At the beginning of the second week, the warriors returned with a canoe carrying several baskets of salt. The baskets contained both the salt gathered from the licks and that from on top of the sand near the river. They were unable to gather the salt without a large mixture of sand. In order to remove the sand from the salt, it was thrown together into certain baskets for the purpose of separating. The baskets were made large at the mouth and small at the bottom. These were set up on a ridge-pole and water was added. Below, vessels were placed to catch the water. It was then strained and placed on the fire to boil, leaving salt at the bottom.

In the cold air, steam from the boiling pots rose in the air. The gathering of salt would do them for the rest of the year until another trip to the licks.

That evening, the smell of venison stew filled the wigwam. To welcome home the warriors, the families came together to share in the preparation and feasting. Tayanita helped Awiagina and Ahyoka prepare the bean bread and winter green onions.

After the meal, Oukonunaka played his flute. The melody lifted into the night sky as Mohe beat the drum. Ahyoka thought of the evening Mr. McCampbell danced his silly jig while her papa played his fiddle. She smiled at the memory and wondered what became of her dear friend, Mary Katherine. Oh, the stories she could tell her.

The cold crept up her knees as the evening drew into early morning. Awiagina had long gone to her bed. Ahyoka and Oukonunaka bid the last of their guests' goodnight and pulled the door to the wigwam closed.

The snowy winter gave way to spring, and the Chota enjoyed a peaceful period.

Chapter 33

May 1779

Ahyoka and Tayanita worked side by side in the garden, tending to the tender shoots of corn, beans, and squash. In the next garden patch, Galilani and her mother tended to the potato and sunflowers. Awiagina sat on a stool outside her wigwam washing the basket of wild onions she'd picked earlier. She was no longer able to work the fields but kept her hands busy with other tasks. She would be needed at the end of summer to help bring babies into the world. Both Ahyoka and Tayanita were with child.

Awiagina had worried Ahyoka was unable to bear a child since she and Oukonunaka had been married over a year. She smiled, happy now, that her worry was for naught.

Ahyoka's sickness lasted a short time, and she enjoyed feeling the flutters in her stomach. She wished her mother was nearby to help with the delivery, as was the way with the white women.

The Chota men left for the spring hunt the month before. The older men and younger boys remained, tending to the village.

The hunting party returned in late June with a canoe loaded with deer skin, beaver pelts, raccoon, and rabbit fur. Meat was cut and dried on drying racks. The skins and furs would be sold to traders to take back to the buyers in the east.

The Council House was filled for the Green Corn festival. Thankful for successful planting of corn and other crops, the village of Chota celebrated the week of the festival with feasts, the Stomp Dance, and games. Ahyoka enjoyed the festival that brought the entire village together to celebrate the harvest of the mainstay to the Cherokee.

Awiagina worked on a large basket to put Ahyoka's baby in when it arrived later in the summer. They grew closer during this time, and Awiagina tried not to worry Ahyoka with her dizzy spells. She had lived sixty-five winters and had only succumbed to bouts with occasional stomach illnesses. The Great Spirit had given her a strong body and spirit.

Oukonunaka and his uncle worked to bring in the harvest of the fields for their families, as did the rest of the village. Ahyoka found the heat took its toll on her, sending her to the shade of the large hickory trees near the fields.

August 17, 1779

Oukonunaka paced outside the wigwam as the squaws came and went. Awiagina finally came to the door, opening it and inviting the new father inside.

His daughter lay next to a sleeping Ahyoka, her tiny fists clenched near her mouth. Her dark hair lay perfect against her small head. He stood, admiring her, unsure what to do with her.

"Ahyoka had a difficult time. She will need to rest, and you will help her." The elder woman gave the order, and Oukonunaka nodded.

"Her name is Kamama," Awiagina said. As was the custom, the grandmother named the child. She remembered hearing Ahyoka say the baby felt like butterflies in her stomach. The name in English means 'butterfly'. Ahyoka wanted to name her after her mother, Christena.

Her Christian name was Christena, but she would be called Kamama.

Tracker stood in the doorway, head cocked, and ears pointed upon hearing the small bird-like cries from the baby. He approached the basket and sniffed the newest member of the family. His tail wagged back and forth, and without further fanfare he curled into a ball beside the basket.

Later that month, Tayanita gave birth to a son, Wohali, meaning Eagle. The child thrived and was of good health. Awiagina had brought both babies into the world as promised. She spent the next weeks helping Ahyoka with Kamama as the other squaws were needed in the fields. She sang old Cherokee songs to pacify the child when her mother had to be away from her.

One afternoon, Ahyoka came in from the field to find Awiagina lying on her pallet. Kamama was sleeping in her basket next to Tracker.

"Grandmother? Are you not well?" Ahyoka knelt down to feel Awiagina's forehead.

"Listen, I want to tell you . . ." her words indistinct and having little strength, she grabbed onto Ahyoka's hand.

"I'm listening, Grandmother." Ahyoka's heartbeat drowned out the elder woman's voice. Ahyoka bent closer to hear.

"You are my granddaughter. I have loved you as my own." Her breathing slowed.

"I love you, Grandmother. Please, rest now." Ahyoka held back the tears, trying to be brave.

"I saw the soldiers and men with long guns coming to our village. You must go."

Ahyoka wasn't sure what Awiagina was talking about. "You saw them, where?"

"The Great Spirit showed me this morning." She gripped Ahyoka's hand tighter. "Go, leave this village."

"Where would we go, Grandmother? We have nowhere to go."

Awiagina's grasp loosened. Ahyoka squeezed her hand.

"Don't go, Grandmother. I need you." The tears flowed, Ahyoka was no longer brave.

"Promise." Awiagina summoned the last of her strength.

"I promise, Grandmother," she whispered. Awiagina's hand fell limp. Ahyoka laid her head on the elder woman's soft bosom and cried.

The following day, Awiagina was buried. Nanye'hi spoke the words over her as she was given back to Mother Earth. Ahyoka held Kamama close, rocking side to side. She thought of all the things Awiagina taught her in the three years she'd lived with her. The village was saddened by her loss.

Ahyoka spoke to Nanye'hi about the words Awiagina spoke before her death. She pleaded with Nanye'hi to speak to the chiefs about leaving Chota and going further south. The chiefs refused.

She spoke to Tayanita. She told her about Awiagina's warning. Her friend didn't want to leave the safety of the village.

"It won't be safe, Tayanita. Grandmother had a vision, and she said we must go."

"I will speak to Mohe." Tayanita knew Awiagina had the gift of visions.

Later, she spoke to Oukonunaka. "We must leave Chota. The British soldiers and white settlers are coming to destroy our village. We must take Kamama and go south to another village. Mr. McKeag talked about Washington County, in North Carolina. That is far enough away."

"I don't know, Ahyoka. What if she was wrong?"

Ahyoka's shoulder sagged. The words Awiagina spoke were a plea.

"I promised her."

The traders who spent the winter in Chota the year before were killed after traveling the road to Charles Towne. Renegade warriors with Dragging Canoe raided settlements from South Carolina to Kentucke since the 1775 Sycamore Shoals treaty. Traders often fell prey to such attacks.

Ahyoka continued her pleading with Oukonunaka to leave the village. She convinced Awiagina's nephew and his wife, along with Oukonunaka's family to leave the village.

Tayanita, Mohe, and her parents also agreed to leave the settlement. Word of attacks in the towns north of Chota prompted the group to leave for Cowee on the Little Tennessee River and Cowee Creek. Nanye'hi had visited the site the year before and confirmed the town had rebuilt after being attacked by the British and white settlers in 1776. The journey, mostly by canoe, would take several weeks, but they would pass many towns along their journey.

On September 2, 1799, six dugout canoes were taken to the river, each holding one family and all their possessions.

Furs, pots, bowls, weapons, bullets, and other sundry items were placed inside, and blessings from the Beloved Woman and Chiefs to carry them safely to Cowee.

Ahyoka thanked Nanye'hi for her kindness. She accepted a medicine pouch with extraordinary beadwork, and sage for protection. The families bid their farewells and embarked on the journey promised by Ahyoka to Awiagina, in the hopes of saving them from attack by the whites.

Chapter 34

September 30th, 1779

For three weeks as the travelers paddled along the Tennessee River, the Great Spirit protected them and brought a bounty of fish and small game to fill their stomachs along the way. Twice they made camp for a night with traders who feared for their lives, but found the Cherokee meant them no harm. They learned of more attacks between settlers and Indians to the south.

Young Oukonunaka proved courageous, and the traders called him "young chief". His uncle kept his rifle close, not trusting the white traders.

The Cherokee village of Cowee sat along the river. The dwellings were more like the cabins Ahyoka remembered at Boonesborough, except they were constructed of wattle and daub, like Chota and Coyatee.

The Chiefs met with the clans at the Council House. Upon the arrival there were twenty-five warriors, squaws, and infants wishing to join the tribe. In all, the families of Oukonunaka, Mohe and Tayanita, and Awiagina's nephew's family settled in the town of Cowee.

Kamama and Wohali, thrived and grew during the fall. Each family constructed a wattle and daub house before the heavy snows arrived.

Ahyoka unpacked her things inside her small cabin. The wooden trunk that Awiagina had gifted her contained all the worldly goods she possessed. The gifts that she received on the day she left the village of Coyatee for Boonesborough in 1777 and her wedding gifts. She held close to her breast the cornhusk doll that Awiagina had given her. It would be handed to her own daughter, Kamama, when she grew old enough to have such things. The wooden slide-top box crafted by her father sat on a shelf Oukonunaka made from the leftover wood from the small table he'd made.

The dwellings were finished before the first snow of 1780 fell. Ahyoka's ink well was once again filled from traders who came from the south. She wrote all that she remembered from the time Kamama was born to this day, January 8th, 1780.

Warriors who came back from hunting, including Mohe and Oukonunaka, learned of the attack on Chota. Nanye'hi and her family were released by the British out of respect, but the rest of the village was taken captive or killed in the raid. Chota was burned to the ground. The War Chief, Oukonunaka's grandfather, perished in the attack. He would be a chief, if the council agreed.

Awiagina's vision was correct. Ahyoka was given credit for saving the twenty-five Cherokee who listened to Awiagina's words and fled Chota.

Nanye'hi left Chota to speak with the white men who wanted to sign another treaty for lands the Cherokee owned to keep peace in the area.

Oukonunaka and Ahyoka lived among the people of Cowee until the Revolutionary War ended. By the time of the Treaty of Paris in 1783, the villages of the Middle Cherokee were part of the new disputed state of Franklin.

Most of the Overhill towns were destroyed during the raids by settlers, causing those who survived to travel south to the mountains in North Carolina.

Hostilities continued between the settlers wanting to rid the Cherokee of their lands and the hundreds of Cherokees still living in the villages along the lower Tennessee River.

Many wanted to settle in the frontier after returning to find their farms and homes destroyed by the British army. The lands that were given to the Cherokee were now in question as to which state had possession.

Although North Carolina laid claim to the land west of the Appalachian Mountains, they were unsure what to do with it. In 1784 the state voted to give the land to the U. S. Congress to pay off their war debts.

Then, after a new election in the North Carolina legislature, the state's representatives changed their mind. They decided to keep the territory. While the representatives went back and forth, the people living in the frontier lived in fear. They thought of the neighboring Cherokee and Chickamaugan's attacking them with no protection from the state of North Carolina.

Not waiting for the state of North Carolina to decide, the settlers took matters into their own hands and voted to form their own state.

On August 23, 1784, upwards of fifty frontiersmen signed a document in the city of Jonesborough declaring their independence from North Carolina. Revolutionary War hero John Sevier headed the loosely organized government of the territory called "Frankland." It was named after a friend of Sevier, a Revolutionary War patriot, Benjamin Franklin. Later the name would be changed to Franklin, to have the backing of Mr. Franklin in securing that the state was accepted into the United States.

Even though Franklin didn't become America's 14th state, it grew at a rapid pace. In late 1785 and early 1786, about ten thousand families moved to the territory from

Virginia and North Carolina. The rogue state expanded to eight counties.

Ahyoka and Oukonunaka and the families who joined them in Cowee now joined other Cherokee who built cabins and began farming. They assimilated to the white culture, hoping to continue to live in peace with the encroaching white settlers.

The winter of 1781, Ahyoka gave birth to Koatohee, a son. In the spring of 1784, she gave birth to her third child, a son. Kanuna. Their Christian names were Jacob and William, respectively.

The village grew in numbers from both southern Cherokee and Overhill Cherokee coming to the area. Oukonunaka, Mohe, and Atsadi traveled to trade with settlers living in Franklin.

Oukonunaka wanted to bring a new cooking skillet and other sundry items for Ahyoka. He spied a white settler who had a cradle sitting on his wagon.

Oukonunaka carried a stack of buckskin and laid it on the back of the wagon.

"How much?" he asked the settler.

"How many bucks do you have there?"

"I bring ten bucks for the cradle. I will bring ten more next spring." Oukonunaka handled the hickory cradle, running his hand over the smooth sides. "Good trade?" He saw on the underside of the cradle a mark he'd seen before.

"Yes, I reckon that'd be a fair trade for a cradle. You have a young one?" the man asked.

"Three," he said, holding up three fingers. "Is that your mark?" Oukonunaka asked.

"Yes, I sign my work with my mark." He extended his hand. "Jacob Diele's my name."

Oukonunaka shook Jacob's hand. He saw a small child, close to the age of Kamama, playing with a wooden doll on the front of his wagon.

"Did you have a daughter, Maggie Diele?" Oukonunaka asked, seeing the look of confusion wash over Jacob's face.

"Yes, our daughter was taken by . . . she was taken in Boonesborough in '76. We survived the attack that summer and left with others to Watauga. Do you know of her?" he asked, the excitement rising in his voice.

"She is my wife." His words fell like a mighty oak, taking the smile off Jacob's face.

"Wife? She is only . . . well, she must be twenty-two now." Tears pooled in Jacob's eyes. "Come, you must meet my wife, Tena. She must know." Jacob motioned for Oukonunaka to get in the back of his wagon.

Oukonunaka turned to Mohe and Atsadi. He spoke to them in Cherokee, telling them to come with him.

At first Jacob wanted to protest, but the other two savages didn't mind riding in the wagon with Oukonunaka. He lifted his daughter to sit on the seat beside him. Oukonunaka smiled at the child, seeing a resemblance to Ahyoka. She quickly turned around, afraid of the painted faces of the Indians.

The ride lasted fifteen minutes over a hilly and rocky wagon road. He pulled in front of a cabin with windows and a large chimney on the side. Oukonunaka, Mohe and Atsadi were told who the man was as they rode to the cabin.

Christena came to the door, seeing the Indians sitting in the wagon behind her daughter. Her mouth opened to scream, but she saw Jacob's hand raise.

"They have news of Maggie. It is good news, Tena." Jacob jumped from the seat, lifting Caroline and putting her down, where she ran to her mother.

"I don't understand. How can this be?" Christena was overcome.

Jacob embraced her, lifting her off the ground. "She is alive, Tena. She is a grown woman."

Christena wiped the tears from her eyes with her apron, not taking her eyes off the three Indians. "Who are they?"

Jacob motioned for the three Indians to get out of the wagon. Oukonunaka spoke to Christena.

"I am Oukonunaka. Ahyoka . . . Maggie Diele, is my woman. She is my wife."

Christena blinked, the words still not able to come out. She looked at Jacob, then back at Oukonunaka.

Oukonunaka recounted her coming to the village and being adopted. He told of her trip over the mountains to be returned to Boonesborough, but they were gone. He explained her coming back to be adopted into the tribe, where she and Oukonunaka were married and now the parents of three children.

"Is she well?" Christena found her words. "Where is your village?"

Oukonunaka thought better than to tell where the village was. "I will bring her to you when I come again to trade."

"You have children?" Christena asked, still in shock over the news of her lost daughter.

"A daughter and two sons."

"This is our daughter, Caroline. Our son, Will, went to fight with the army. He was taken from us at Kings Mountain." Jacob's voice showed the raw emotion of the recent death.

"You asked about my mark, on the cradle. How do you know of this mark?" Jacob asked.

"A trader, Klumpf, gave a wooden box with your mark to Ahyoka when we were at Chota."

"Oh yes, the Quaker. He was killed not far from here in '78." Jacob remembered his body being found and buried outside the settlement. Jacob didn't realize there was a letter to him and Christena in his jacket. The arrow had pierced the letter and his heart.

"I will take the cradle to Ahyoka. She will want to come back to see you."

After feeding the three Indians, Jacob took them back to where they left their canoe.

He took from his jacket a doll, the one Caroline held back at the cabin. "This was Maggie's. Please take it to her," he said.

Oukonunaka wrapped it carefully in a rabbit skin. The cradle was wrapped in a wool blanket and set inside the canoe.

After the warriors made their trades and loaded the canoe, Oukonunaka raised his hand to Jacob. He smiled as they paddled the canoe away from the bank. He would have a story to tell Ahyoka and the children when he came back to the cabin, a wonderful story.

Discussion Questions

1. Jacob Diele heard about the Transylvania Company offering tracts of land to settlers in 1775. Could he have migrated to Kentucky as the story suggests?

—This is true, the Treaty of Sycamore Shoals in 1775 opened up new lands in what was then the hunting grounds of the Cherokee and other tribes in the area. In 1775 the Overhill Cherokee were persuaded at the Treaty of Sycamore Shoals to sell an enormous tract of land in central Kentucky. Although this agreement with the Transylvania Land Company violated British law, it nevertheless became the basis for the white takeover of that area.

2. Did Daniel Boone lead the Diele family and others in the story into Kentucky?

—While Daniel Boone led people into Kentucky, the Diele family was fictional.

In April of 1775, while working for Richard Henderson's Transylvania Company, Boone directed colonists to an area in Kentucky he named Boonesborough, where he set up fort to claim the settlement from the Indians. That same year he brought his own family west to live on the settlement and became its leader.

3. Did Jemima Boone, Betsy and Frances Callaway really get kidnapped?

Even though the capture of Maggie Diele is fiction, the kidnapping of the other girls is true. On July 14, 1776, a raiding party caught three teenage girls from Boonesborough as they were floating in a canoe on the Kentucky River. They were Jemima, daughter of Daniel Boone, and Elizabeth and Frances, daughters of Colonel Richard Callaway. The Cherokee Hanging Maw led the raiders, two Cherokee and three Shawnee warriors. The girls' capture raised alarm and

Boone organized a rescue party. Meanwhile, the captors hurried the girls north toward the Shawnee towns across the Ohio River. They were rescued three days later by Boone and his search party. The capture and rescue of the girls is the basis for the book, The Last of the Mohicans, by James Fenimore Cooper, in 1826.

4. Was there really a Beloved Woman named Nancy Ward, Nanye'hi?

—Yes, Nanye'hi was born in the Cherokee town of Chota. She was named the Beloved Woman after her first husband, Kingfisher, was killed in battle. She picked up his rifle and continued fighting, rallying the Cherokee to win the battle. She had a son, Five Killer,

—While the association with Maggie Diele is fictional, Nanye'hi was really married to Bryant Ward, and she did save Lydia Bean from death, as the story states. She was also spared, along with her family, when the settlers and British attacked Chota in 1780.

5. The title, This Dark and Bloody Ground, has long been disputed as to who said it, and when. The title of this book was taken from the following quote:

"You have bought a fair land, but there is a cloud hanging over it; you will find its settlement dark and bloody." Attributed to Chief Dragging Canoe, 1775

—On March 15, 1775, during the second day of negotiations, the Transylvania Company proposed to purchase most of what is now Kentucky and middle Tennessee from Tsalagis. In response to Yonega negotiator Richard Henderson's proposals, Tsi'yu-gunsini, who was considered an obscure warrior from the Overhills, walked to the center of the treaty grounds and spoke:

"Whole nations have melted away in our presence like balls of snow before the sun, and have scarcely left their names behind, except as imperfectly recorded by their enemies and destroyers. It was once hoped that your people would not be willing to travel beyond the mountains, so far from the ocean, on which your commerce was carried on, and your connections maintained with the nations of Europe. But now that fallacious hope has vanished; you have passed the mountains and settled upon the Tsalagi lands and wish to have your usurpations sanctioned by the confirmation of a treaty. When that should be obtained, the same encroaching spirit will lead you upon other lands of the Tsalagis. New cessions will be applied for, and finally the country which the Tsalagis and our forefathers have so long occupied will be called for; and a small remnant of this nation, once so great and formidable, will be compelled to seek a retreat in some far distant wilderness, there we will all dwell but a short space of time before we will again behold the advancing banners of the same greedy host; who, not being able to point out any farther retreat for the miserable Tsalagis, would then proclaim the extinction of the whole race". After delivering his prophetic oration, Dragging Canoe left the negotiations, which prompted younger warriors to withdraw as well. Despite his best efforts, Dragging Canoe saw that the Tsalagi Peace Chiefs were still willing to make a deal for the purchase of large sections of Tsalagi territory.

At the conclusion of the land cession negotiations, Dragging Canoe turned to Henderson and said: "You have bought a fair land, but you will find its settlement dark and bloody."'

Jeff Corntassel-

http://www. corntassel. net/contact. htm

Dragging Canoe, RESPONSE TO TREATY OF SYCAMORE SHOALS (1775). Text courtesy of http://www. corntassel. net/

Acknowledgements

For my precious grandchildren, Haden, Hadley, Gibson, Iyla, Lydia, Griffin, Adalyn, and Nash: I hope someday you will enjoy American history and family history as much as I do.

A heartfelt thank you to my mother, Janet Hughes Crecelius Johnson, for instilling the love of family history in me from a young age. Thank you for making sure to include some place historical on each of the summer vacations you and Dad planned.

Thank you to my husband, Doug, for going on wild goose chases and discovering wonderful places with me on the quest for research.

I would like to thank the various Park Rangers and re-enactors for their help in locating information or giving valuable historical information at the Cumberland Gap National Park, Martin's Station Historical Park, and The Wilderness Road State Park.

Thank you, Grace Augustine, for taking on my project again!

I'm thankful for teachers who inspired me at a young age to love both Indiana history as well as United States history. Thank you, Russell Poe and Rita Davis.

And thank you, dear reader, for choosing my book to read. I hope you will find enjoyment within the pages.

About the Author

Lori Roberts is an educator, historian, author, and presenter for historical events and workshops. She has taught for thirty years. Currently, Lori teaches United States History at the Middle School level. She presents the personas of Mrs. General Thomas "Stonewall" Jackson (Mary Anna Morrison Jackson), as well as Corrie Ten Boom, Concentration Camp survivor, the 1st First Lady of Indiana, Ann Gilmore Hay Jennings, and First Lady Martha Washington.

Lori is an author of historical fiction and paranormal/mystery, having four titles published. Lost Letters and Willow are available through major book sellers in both the United States and abroad and through Warren Publishing Company. The Lowcountry Ghost Trilogy, published by Crecelius Haus Publishing, includes Cries in the Night~A Lowcountry Ghost Story, Book 1, and Where the Sweetgrass Grows, book 2. Both are available through major book sellers in both the United States and abroad.

Currently, Lori is writing the second book in the American Frontier Series, Remember My Name ~ White Owl's Tale.

Lori's books are also available through her website, www. loriroberts.com.

Lori lives in rural southern Indiana with her husband, Doug. She has three grown children and nine grandchildren. She and her husband also have three Golden Retrievers, Maggie, Rhett and Rowan, and a cat, Jerry Lee.

Connect with Lori Roberts

Connect with Lori Roberts:
author_loriroberts@yahoo.com
https://www.loriroberts.com/
https://twitter.com/stonewallswife
http://authorloriroberts.blogspot.com/
iamlorirobertsinstagram.com
author_loriroberts amazon. com/Lori-Roberts/e/B0089A94EG

Lori Roberts loves to hear from her readers. If you have a question regarding the story or any of the characters, send your questions to her Facebook page, https://www. facebook.com/Stonewallswife/ OR email her at author_ loriroberts@yahoo. com

www.ingramcontent.com/pod-product-compliance
Lightning Source LLC
Chambersburg PA
CBHW020326110726
47898CB00003B/767